Praise for *Part of the World*

"Reading *Part of the World* by Robert Lopez felt to me like standing in front of one of those marvelous, mind-bending exhibits at the Museum of Jurassic Technology that seem at first glance to be doing exactly nothing and at second glance to be dissolving and reconstituting reality as we thought we knew it. Literary pleasures like this are all too uncommon."
—Laird Hunt

"The prose found in Robert Lopez's new novel, *Part of the World*, is as flat as this piece of paper but as deep as the deepest well. The world this world is a part of is an affectless poetics planet caught in the black-hole gravity of a Stephen Dixon-esque free-falling narrative sink. Stranger than *The Stranger*, it is a relentless, droll, blinkless, book."
—Michael Martone

"*Part of the World* is a gripping read, ominous, blackly hilarious and psychologically acute. ... Distinctive in its ability to weave metafictional games about language, psychological investigations into repetition and trauma, genuine suspense, and droll humor, *Part of the World* merits a wide readership."
—Jason Jones, from review in *Mid-American Review*

"Beyond any discussion of occurrence in *Part of the World*, though, the real treasure here is Lopez's writing. He's so in control of his character's voice and the layering of thought that to call him a more pleasantly imbibed Beckett seems precise. *Part of the World* is a book to be read with delight and wonder—and some slight miffing that it's over."
—Blake Butler, from review in *Rain Taxi*

"In his first novel, Robert Lopez leads the reader into a peculiar "part of the world" on his own terms. The novel itself deals with the everyday actions of the narrator, from renting an apartment to buying a used car. However, these tasks become yard sticks by which one must measure the narrator himself and his sense of reality. By the end of the novel, the reader is forced to question the validity of everything the narrator has said, as a new, obfuscated yet elucidated reality begins to appear."
—Leigh Murphy, from review in *Verse*

"The narrator's neuroses are, at first, unremarkable, but they intensify and the result is a snowballing effect, an imperceptible building of madness and memory that takes on a distinctly sinister aspect that was only hinted at in earlier pages."
—Jeff Waxman, from review in *The Review of Contemporary Fiction*

"As a revelation, then, of the ultimate emptiness on which we all levitate, Lopez's book succeeds wonderfully. It succeeds even more wonderfully as a textual trace of the movement of consciousness …"
—Matthew Roberson, from review in *American Book Review*

"*Part of the World* is full of trickery and dark humor. Manic, mindbinding, musical—and always masterful."
—John Reed

KAMBY BOLONGO MEAN RIVER

KAMBY BOLONGO MEAN RIVER

a novel

Robert Lopez

DZANC
BOOKS

DZANC
BOOKS

1334 Woodbourne Street
Westland, MI 48186

www.dzancbooks.org

Copyright © 2009, Text by Robert Lopez

Published 2009 by Dzanc Books
Book design by Steven Seighman

Portions of this book have appeared in *New York Tyrant*, *Unsaid*, and *Willow Springs*

06 07 08 09 10 11 5 4 3 2 1
First edition September 2009

ISBN-13: 978-0-9767177-6-8

Printed in the United States of America

Also by Robert Lopez

Part of the World

Should the phone ring I will answer it. I will say the hello how are you and wait for a response. I will listen to what the person on the other end says. I will listen to the words. Sometimes I don't listen. Sometimes I wait until the person finishes answering the hello how are you so I can say whatever it is I'd been saying to myself before the phone rang.

What I say to myself usually starts with the hello how are you then I'm fine I have a headache I didn't sleep last night.

I am fine means I do not have a headache. I cannot be fine and have a headache at the same time and I don't think anyone else can either. In this way I am like most people in this way I am like anyone. If I have a headache I am not fine and if I am not fine I probably didn't sleep last night.

I was not born with a headache but I don't think I was born fine. Why I think this is because of what I heard Charlie and Mother talking about one day when we were children.

Should the phone ring I will answer and the conversation will stop there. Saying I'm fine is no way to start a conversation or keep one going.

What I am fine means is please stop talking.

Should the phone ring I might let it keep ringing until the machine answers. This way I will not have to bother with listening or the words. Sometimes I have trouble with both. Sometimes I do good with the listening but forget the words and sometimes it's the other way around.

The trouble is when I listen I don't listen for the words. I listen for what is between the words and behind them. The way you do this is to listen to how the voice sounds. If you concentrate on the words you lose the voice and the voice is always too important to lose. How the voice pronounces each word is probably the most important thing.

The words themselves are important less than half the time.

When I concentrate on the words I have trouble understanding what they mean. If I understand one word I don't understand the word that follows. I have trouble understanding what one word has to do with another.

For instance I don't know what happy has to do with birthday or good with morning.

What you have to do is understand how people use words and go from there.

The trouble is some people use words one way but other people use those same words a different way altogether. My problem is I think about one word for too long. A caller will say a word like injury and I will think about the word injury for a minute or two and not hear the other words. I won't know who has the injury or why it matters. This always happens to me and this is why should the phone ring I might let it keep ringing until the machine answers.

A word like injury can split your head open.

Should the phone ring a decision will have to be made and this is always the case. And once one decision is made you have to make another right after it and your life becomes a series of decisions about the telephone and how to conduct yourself over it.

Only answering machines can do listening and the words at the same time. This is why answering machines are the best things going. I don't know what life was like before answering machines or how people got along with themselves without them.

The sound between words can be great or small or great and small at the same time.

The sound between words can be troubling or comforting but almost never at the same time so this is probably beside the point.

I think I have lived an entire life beside the point but even this is probably beside the point.

This is why the sound between words is always better to listen to than the words themselves.

Charlie and I were the children and Mother was the mother and this is how you can tell everyone apart.

Also Charlie was older which meant he was responsible.

Injury sounds like a place like Injury Alaska. Like the people of Injury Alaska fish and hunt and trade with their neighbors and the average lifespan of an Injured Alaskan is 58 years. This is what I think of when I hear a word like injury.

Then I'll think about someone in a jury like judge and jury or a jury of your peers. I'll think about the ladies and gentlemen of the jury and the deliberation causing a hung jury. I have never myself been in a jury or on a jury and have never said a phrase like the jury is still out on that one. The jury is never out that long even when they have hung themselves.

This is why it's always better to listen to the voice and leave the words alone.

Not sleeping last night always gives me a headache but not the same as thinking about a word like injury. The not sleeping last night headache feels like when they give you too many pills.

Mother would give me pills every morning when I woke and every night when I went to bed. She would spread them out in her hand so that they made different shapes. Her favorites were pill circles and squares. Sometimes the pill circles and squares were bigger or smaller depending on how many pills I needed at the time. I would take the pills one by one off Mother's hand and she would encourage me to make the circle or square disappear. When I was done she would say good boy and kiss my forehead and then tuck me in goodnight.

The pills themselves were different sizes and shapes and colors. Mother never said which pill was which or what any of them were for.

My favorites were the blue and pink ones. The blue one was a tiny oval and had the letter P carved into it. I used to wonder if that was someone's job to carve the letter P into the blue pills.

The pink one was shaped like a submarine and had no letters carved into it. There were two lines across either the top or bottom depending on which end you swallowed first.

I tried not to taste the pills but sometimes I couldn't help it.

Sometimes I would choke on the pink ones and Mother would have to slap my back for me. She would slap me twice and I would either swallow the pill or spit it up and have to start over.

She never had to do the Heimlich maneuver on me. She would say this she would say don't make me have to do the Heimlich maneuver on you.

The pink ones were awful and if she ever had to do the Heimlich maneuver on me it was because of the pink ones.

Not sleeping last night is another reason answering machines are the best things going. Whenever I didn't sleep last night I never answer the phone the next day. Maybe this would be different if there were no answering machines in the world but it's good we can thank God and never know.

I will lay me down to sleep and everything is fine for a minute or two. My head on the pillow is fine and my body under the blankets is also fine.

I always start off face up on my back and I look at the ceiling and tell myself I am tired and should go to sleep.

I tell myself millions of people are falling asleep right now and I should be one of them.

I will close my eyes and wait for myself to fall asleep and when nothing happens I tell myself I'm not sleeping again so now what.

This is when I usually count the holes in the ceiling tile. I will count the holes in every tile to see which ones have the most holes.

Mother said only certain kinds of people have trouble sleeping like musical geniuses and serial killers. Then she would say which one are you going to be and of course she was right.

I like it best when I call someone and the answering machine answers. I like it how the phone keeps ringing with no one picking up and you wonder is someone going to pick up the phone. You wonder if no one is home and this is why the phone keeps ringing or if someone is home but doesn't feel like talking.

There is nothing wrong with not wanting to talk because the person probably didn't sleep last night and has a headache.

This is why we all should thank God for answering machines. We should thank God for inventing answering machines and allowing us to have them in our homes.

God created answering machines the same way he created Alaska the same way he created dogs so that we as people wouldn't have to do it ourselves. We as people don't have the time to come up with something like an answering machine the same as Alaska.

I like it when the phone keeps ringing and you hope the answering machine answers and you say to yourself please don't pick up the phone please don't pick up the phone and then the machine finally answers and you know it is the machine by the way the machine pauses before saying thank you for calling I am not home right now I have a headache but if you leave your name and number I might call you back soon.

Should the phone ring I will ask the caller to identify themselves before I say the hello how are you. The machine can also do this but not with the same authority. This is not the machine's fault. The machine was not programmed to have this kind of authority. God knows if the machine has this kind of authority there would be even more trouble than there already is.

Otherwise the machine is perfect and can do no wrong.

Should the phone ring I will say please identify yourself like that. I will try to sound like a military policeman or security guard when I say please identify yourself because MPs and security guards speak with authority. I will say this right after I pick up the phone. I will not say who is calling please because I do not like the way that sounds. Another reason I will not say who is calling please is because a military policeman or security guard would never say who is calling please. Only people who are not military policemen or security guards would say something like this. How I present myself on the phone is important and saying something like who is calling please is not what I want to do with myself.

When I have a headache it is hard for me to say please identify yourself the way a military policeman or security guard would.

It is hard for me to sleep here too which is why I almost always have a headache now.

I have not always wanted to sound like a military policeman or security guard. There were times I wanted to sound like a boxing trainer. I'm not sure why I would've wanted to sound like a boxing trainer other than to say I used to watch boxing on the television. I liked it how the fat trainers would stand outside the ropes and yell and scream at the boxer inside the ring. I liked it how they had a towel draped over their shoulder and would curse the referee.

I've never boxed myself because it was too rough. I might get hurt. It was important when I was growing up that I not get hurt.

Charlie and I would watch the boxing on television together Friday nights. Mother would be out of the house doing God knows what those Friday nights we watched boxing.

Sometimes she would bring us home a dinner of sandwiches and coleslaw and whenever she did this we thanked her by eating all of it and not looking up.

MPs and security guards get hurt sometimes but for them it is probably okay. For them it is part of the job. Only MPs and security guards can have a headache and be fine at the same time.

I don't think I've ever known an MP or security guard but I have seen them on the TV. They are always handsome in their uniforms. Almost anyone is handsome in a uniform MPs and security guards especially.

For me it is not okay to get hurt. I think if I were to get hurt I might die. No one ever said this to me out loud but I remember hearing Charlie and Mother talking about it. I was in my room and Charlie and Mother were in the kitchen talking about how I could die if I got hurt. They didn't say why I would die if I got hurt but Mother seemed especially concerned this would happen. The way she sounded it sounded like I could get hurt and die from eating an ice cream cone.

I never asked Charlie or Mother why I would die if I got hurt because I don't think I was supposed to know. I think it was a secret between Charlie and Mother.

Mother gave birth to Charlie and me and she would tell us this every few days.

I think she thought we would forget if she didn't remind us.

She would say I gave birth to you like that. Usually she would point at the two of us and move her finger back and forth when she said I gave birth to you. Charlie and I would agree with her by nodding and looking at the floor.

This was probably the first time I couldn't understand what words had to do with each other.

I could understand when Mother gave us a sandwich and coleslaw or gave me my pills because she made the sandwich and coleslaw herself or took the pills out of the box and made a pill circle or square for me.

Mother said she went through hell to give birth to us. She said she was in labor for two days each time. She said it tore her insides out and that she was in horrible agony the whole time.

What I remember was that it only took her a few minutes to make me a sandwich or give me my pills. This is why I think she was exaggerating about giving birth to us like that.

This is also why whenever she said happy birthday to us I didn't believe her.

I only heard Charlie and Mother talking about me getting hurt and dying that one time. I was sure they'd talked about it other times but not with me there to overhear them.

Charlie himself was allowed to get hurt but Mother made Charlie promise to make sure I didn't. She told him he was responsible and that I was his responsibility.

So far I have lived a whole life without getting hurt and then dying.

This is where I should probably say thank you Charlie but why bother.

Uniforms are always good and I have always enjoyed wearing uniforms whenever I was allowed to wear one. I got to wear a baseball uniform one summer because they let me join the team. I think I wanted to join the football team but I was told it was too rough which meant I might get hurt and die. I never saw anyone get hurt and die playing football. I saw players get hurt and carted off the field but none of them ever died I don't think.

Why uniforms are good is this way you don't have to worry about what to wear yourself. For instance I like it now that I have a uniform and don't have to worry about what to wear every day. One less thing to worry about is something I've heard all kinds of people say.

The uniform I wear now is comfortable but not as handsome as my old baseball uniform. My old baseball uniform was made from a fabric they call polyester. Polyester is the best fabric to make uniforms out of.

The uniform I wear now is made from cotton which is not nearly as good to make uniforms out of as polyester is.

Polyester is one of the great words and I never have any trouble with it.

The only trouble with this uniform is I sweat too much in it. Everyday I sweat right through the uniform and they have to bring me a fresh one. I always sweat too much and when I sweat too much I chafe and when I chafe the insides of my thighs are rubbed raw.

I tell them it's hard for me to walk around like this which is why they give me powder sometimes. They don't give me powder like Mother did because Mother knew how much I chafed too.

It is hard to say which is better uniforms or answering machines.

No one looks as handsome in a uniform as a military policeman or security guard. Baseball players don't even compare to MPs or security guards.

The people who bring me powder are the same ones who bring the uniforms. I can't tell how many uniforms they have for me. Every three or four days they take my uniform and give me a different one. This different uniform looks exactly like the other one so they're not as different as you'd think. They are the same uniform only different versions.

Maybe there's a better way to say this but here is the trouble with words.

I think they're washing one while I'm wearing the other is what I want to say. I think it takes three or four days for them to wash uniforms here.

Only once or twice did they take a uniform from me and not give me a replacement. They left me naked for two or three days each time.

There was nothing to distract myself from myself those days and they knew it.

I asked them what am I supposed to do now and they said it's one less thing to worry about.

If I had a list of things to worry about the phone ringing and how to conduct myself over it would be at the top. After that it's the air conditioning and then the uniforms.

They tell me I look nice in my uniform whenever they bring me a new one and who can argue with them.

I'm sure MPs and security guards have different versions of the same uniform too. I'm sure they don't have only one uniform to wear every day on patrol. They are probably washing one while wearing the other like everyone else does.

I don't think I myself have ever worked as an MP or security guard. I don't think I myself have ever worked. I think I may have wanted to once but was not allowed for one reason or another.

Why I will ask people to identify themselves is because sometimes I have callers ask for people who aren't here. I don't know why callers think those people are here when I am the only one who is ever here. I am here all the time and there is never anyone here with me. As far as I know I am the only one who has ever been here.

There was no here before me is another way of saying it.

Here is the sort of place that should have a military policeman or security guard standing outside the door. They should patrol up and down for intruders.

Here is a room with four walls and one window. The window does not look out into the real world like most windows. There are no trees or birds out the window and there's no grass or sunlight either. Worst of all there is no river out the window.

This window is like a mirror and this is how they watch me. They are on the other side of the window keeping an eye on me for my own good.

I cannot see them watching me which is probably another good thing.

Otherwise I would spend my whole day watching them watch me.

I have a comfortable bed here with three pillows. I use one pillow for my head another for between my legs and the last one to wrap my arms around.

Intruders can be anyone so the MPs or security guards would have to be vigilant. Doctors in their white coats and clipboards are intruders the same as a burglar would be. Even Charlie and Mother would look like intruders to an MP or security guard. This is why you need MPs and security guards patrolling up and down outside your door at all times. They protect you from every sort of intruder.

Should the phone ring it might be an intruder on the other end.

Calling someone on the phone is an intrusion though most callers don't think of it this way. Most callers go right into the hello how are you and never once apologize for intruding. This is why whenever I make a call I say right off that I am sorry for intruding and then I beg forgiveness. Only then will I say the hello how are you I'm fine I have a headache I didn't sleep last night.

I only apologize for intruding when a person answers the phone themselves as opposed to the machine doing it for them. I would apologize to the machine but the machine is never sorry for the intrusion. The machine welcomes all intruders equally. The machine looks forward to all intruders and does not pass judgment on any of them. This is another reason machines are the best things going.

The machine would never have you beg forgiveness either.

Should the phone ring it might be Charlie on the other end.

More than likely though it will not be Charlie on the other end because Charlie does not like to intrude on people.

Sometimes uniforms come with hats or helmets but just as often not. Hats and helmets aren't necessary for any uniform to look good but they can help. If there were MPs or security guards patrolling outside my door they wouldn't themselves need hats or helmets.

I didn't like wearing my baseball hat but they said I couldn't play without it. They said it was part of being on the team. I didn't like the way my hat made my hair look and I wouldn't have liked the way it looked whether I was on a team or not. I had curly hair when I played baseball but now I am bald like a baby's bottom like an eagle.

I remember when Charlie and I wanted to go to a private school because of the uniforms. They also had a boxing team which is another reason Charlie wanted to go there. I didn't care so much about the boxing team because why bother but Charlie did and that was fine with me. We saw these uniforms around the neighborhood and found out which private school had them but when we asked Mother about it she said we all had to make sacrifices so the answer was no.

Why we also wanted to go to this private school was because of the security guards. This private school had security guards at both entrances and Charlie and I would test them whenever we could. We'd climb over the fence and walk into the school like we were regular students but the guards always stopped us and chased us away.

Because we didn't have uniforms made it easy for them to spot us.

Instead we would go to our public school in our regular clothes which didn't look anything like uniforms. What we'd wear is blue jeans and t-shirts but I always had to wear Charlie's old blue jeans and t-shirts because he was older and Mother couldn't afford my own jeans and t-shirts. She didn't have to tell me about sacrifices this time because I wasn't as dumb as I looked back then.

That was something Mother would say to both me and Charlie all the time. Whenever one of us would do something right around the house like clean up the kitchen or make our beds Mother would thank us by saying you're not as dumb as you look.

After school we'd come home and do our homework at the kitchen table. I always needed help with my homework and it was math especially. I had trouble with fractions and square roots which were two more words I didn't know what they had to do with each other.

I would be in class and the teacher would ask us what the square root of some number was and while all the students were scribbling the answers I would think about the word square for a few minutes and how that square was a perfect shape like a circle which is why Mother would make pill circles and squares and I was always happy to make them disappear for her.

So whenever the teacher walked by my desk and saw my blank paper she would punish me with her stick. Then she'd ask me why I didn't do the problem and I said I didn't know. She would say how can you not know why you didn't do the problem and I would answer by saying I don't know that either. This is when she'd punish me with her stick again and send me home.

Charlie needed help with his homework too but Mother wasn't home to help us and by the time she did get home she was tired of making sacrifices.

I don't like disappointing callers so sometimes I pretend to be the person they are trying to call. This is what separates me from most callers. I figure it's the least I can do for the people who call me.

This is the kind of thing Charlie himself would do too. When we were kids we'd pretend to be all kinds of people. For two whole summers Charlie pretended to be a boxer and I pretended to be his trainer. Every morning we'd wake up while it was still dark out and go jogging. I think Mother was still asleep in her room when we did this otherwise she probably wouldn't have allowed it. If Mother knew we were doing this she'd probably think I might get hurt and die from it.

Charlie would do the jogging and I'd hold onto the rope we tied around him and follow behind on a skateboard. It was like Charlie was a horse and I was a buggy which is something we never pretended to be. Charlie didn't like animals growing up which meant I wasn't allowed to like them either. But we saw some boxer and trainer do this horse and buggy maneuver in a movie one time so we thought we could do it too. We'd jog all the way to the ice cream truck on the other side of town and back. What we wouldn't do is buy a Popsicle or ice cream cone because we were in training. Sometimes Mother would give us money for the ice cream truck but most times she would say we all had to make sacrifices when we asked her about money for the ice cream truck.

Then we'd go into the basement after the jog and I'd hold a laundry bag up so he could pummel it to death. Then I'd make him a breakfast drink of raw eggs and milk and he'd drink it right up and only once or twice did he throw up from it. Charlie didn't mind throwing up because boxers threw up all the time.

I can't remember if Charlie ever actually boxed another boxer inside a ring. I'm sure he would've wanted to otherwise what did we do all that training for. This is something Charlie probably regrets to this very day.

It probably haunts him that he never became a real boxer and this is probably why Charlie is the way he is.

This is why I feel sorry for Charlie sometimes.

We watched the boxing matches Friday nights and we'd watch boxing movies when there were no matches on. We were boxing crazy for two whole summers and each of us bought our own trunks and mouthpieces and we made Charlie's bedroom into a ring. We made ropes out of the fox and raccoon stoles from Mother's closet and we used her old music box for a bell. We stapled all those stoles together and took the bell out of the box and Mother gave us hell when she found out about it. She gave more hell to Charlie because he was older and responsible and I remember feeling bad for Charlie that his own mother wanted to kill him like that.

Mother never wanted to kill me herself I don't think.

Sometimes Mother gave us hell by making us read the dictionary. She would have us sit down at the kitchen table and read the dictionary together. We would pass the dictionary back and forth and have to memorize certain words and later she would come home and test us.

She would have us do all the Hs in one sitting for instance.

Another thing Charlie and I would do together is riddles. I would tell Charlie that if he wanted to be a boxer he'd have to think on his feet and riddles help with this. I told him all boxers should do riddles and he was no exception. So I would say to Charlie that if a plane crashed on the border of Alaska and Canada where do you bury the survivors. Then I would tell him what walks on four in the morning two in the afternoon and three in the evening.

Charlie would answer what does that have to do with boxing and he was right of course.

This is why I like to pretend when callers call for people who aren't me. There is no right way to do this but it helps if you can make yourself believe you are the actual person you are pretending to be.

No matter who it is I am pretending to be I always sound like a military policeman or security guard. This would be fine except sometimes I am trying not to sound like an MP or security guard. Sometimes I've wanted to sound like a boxing trainer but other times I want to sound like anyone. The way you try to sound like anyone is to sound like you are falling asleep while speaking. The way to do this is to speak slowly and mumble and the longer you're at it you speak even more slowly and mumble more. This is the same way drunk people talk and the same as people who have been given too many pills.

One time I asked a caller if I sounded like an MP or security guard but the caller hung up before answering. I took this to mean yes I did sound like an MP or security guard.

What I never do is try to sound like a doctor in a white coat and clipboard. No one likes doctors in person and even less over the phone.

The people who bring me the powder and uniforms are doctors in white coats and clipboards.

These are the same ones who watch me from the other side of the window.

Along with my bed I have a table and chairs in here with me. Sometimes when they want to talk with me we all sit around the table together and it's nice.

I know it's nice because once we get settled in our chairs around the table one of them always says isn't this nice.

Then one of us will say something and the others have to respond like it's an actual conversation.

One of the doctors will say how are you feeling today and I will say I'm fine which means please stop talking.

Then we all look at each other like it's a contest as to who will say what first.

Sometimes this goes on for a while and it doesn't bother me like it does them.

Then they might say something like how was your breakfast this morning.
I might say it was delicious.
They might say what did they bring you.
I might say the usual.
And they might say which is what.
I might say I'm afraid I don't remember.

One of them is always quiet and scribbling in a notebook whenever we do this.

He is the one I usually tell to go fuck himself when he has a chance.

I will say to him go fuck yourself when you get a chance like that.

This is when they all say we'll see you later which means they are going behind the window to either watch me again or go fuck themselves.

This is what professional actors do so well. Professional actors say when they are acting they literally become the character they are playing. So if an actor named Charlie Robertson is playing a military policeman Charlie Robertson becomes an MP on stage in front of the audience. There is no Charlie Robertson on stage during the performance is another way of saying it. A skilled actor can convince an audience of this every time and if the hypothetical Charlie Robertson is a skilled actor then we can assume the audience believes he is actually a military policeman on that stage during the performance. What happens to Charlie Robertson during this time we don't know. We don't know where he goes or what he does when he gets there.

In some ways it is like death it is like what happens to you when you die.

In this way you could call actors killers. You could say that acting is a kind of killing which it certainly is.

Should the phone ring and the caller asks for someone who is not me the first thing I'll do is imagine how that person might talk and go from there. It's better if it sounds like the person they ask for works as an MP or security guard but it rarely happens that way. What does happen is they ask for some name I've never heard before. Some name that could never belong to an MP or security guard.

How Mother tested us was she'd sit down at the kitchen table and ask us questions.

Charlie always went first because he was older and Mother made me go into the living room to wait my turn.

Mother would say how do you spell a word like harassment.
Charlie would say h a r r a s s m e n t.
Mother would say you're wrong again Charlie.
Mother would say if you don't know how to spell it then what does it mean.
Charlie would say it means when someone bothers you all the time.

Then it would be my turn and Mother would ask me how do you spell harbinger.

This is when I told her that I knew harassment so she should've asked me that instead.

Should the phone ring it might be the intruder who calls here sometimes. This last time he called I wasn't even finished with the hello how are you when he said there were too many people there when it happened so I decided to cut some of them.
So I said when what happened.
Then he said for instance Arthur Wheeler was there but had absolutely nothing to do with it. Gil Figgitz had no idea what the hell was going on so why put him in.
I said you tell me.
He said basically all June Harrison does is take up space wherever she goes and this was no exception.
I said that Mother used to say the same thing about Charlie whenever he gave her his report card to sign.

Instead of asking me about Mother or Charlie the intruder kept on and said I know for a fact Judy Jakker wanted nothing to do with it. She told me so in that grating accent of hers so out of respect for Judy I'll say she wasn't even there. Betty Lager is an easy cut despite her obvious physical attributes.

This is something Charlie does himself. We will have a conversation and I will try to ask him questions but he never answers. You don't know if it's because Charlie is deaf or an idiot which is why this intruder reminds me so much of Charlie.

I don't think this intruder is Charlie though because I would probably recognize Charlie's voice.

This is when I said who the fuck are these people and finally the intruder said something that made sense.

The intruder said you know damn well who these people are. I said do I now.

Then he went on and said Frank Pugo shouldn't have been mixed up in this in the first place and his role from what I understand was minimal. William Shedd doesn't need this kind of recognition given his situation. As far as Harriet Dovovich is concerned it's best to leave well enough alone. Donnie Walker wasn't there at all but he's my friend and he'd be excited to know he was included. Dottie Western was there but only for a few minutes. She left her turquoise Indian bracelet so I have to call her. Pugo's mother was there but I don't think she was involved although it wouldn't surprise me.

By this time I think I said to myself this is definitely not Charlie talking. First of all Charlie doesn't know this many people and never would. Also Charlie doesn't talk like this. Charlie needs time to think about what he's saying and he could never say all this without thinking about it for a very long time.

Then I decided it was the security guard from the private school that chased Charlie and me away all the time.

So the security guard said I'd like to say Bennie Mangine was there and responsible for the whole thing but I'd be lying. Considering what Jenn Untermeyer did for me the night of Bill Shedd's going away party there's no way I can put her in the middle of this. Along those same lines Grace Heaney gets a pass too. Of course Sam Marichino was in it up to his ears but given his condition.

This is when I said I have to go now they have to give me my pills.

Then the security guard said it's almost finished and then we can both hang up on each other.

He went on to say Fran Pollo was acting awfully strange so maybe she'll stay in I'm not sure. She did let me feel her up when we were sixteen so I'm sure I owe her something. Denise Livingston never seemed quite right to me. Her eyes are too far apart from each other. Sal Gonzalez saved my ass once. We were getting on a train and I was drunk and not paying attention and I stepped into the gap and Sal grabbed my arm and kept me from breaking my ass. So regardless of the possibility that Sal may have been responsible I could never name him.

I said how could you again so he would feel like this was an actual conversation and I was playing the part of somebody he was talking to.

Then he said at any rate those are the people I'm cutting. I'm not sure if it'll make a difference. By the time the cops got there it was out of our hands. I'm not sure who called them. The one with the mustache said what's the problem here and I said there's no problem. Then he said well someone has a problem and then the other one said does it have something to do with and I said yes officer it does.

This is when we hung up on each other.

After he said yes officer it does I said can we hang up on each other now and he said yes.

I don't know what this intruder meant by cutting the people and I don't know why he told me all this in the first place.

Should the phone ring I will say who are you cutting and what does it have to do with me.

Charlie would get himself cut all the time because he was a boxer so this is why I thought this was Charlie and something happened to his voice.

The one cut that gave Charlie the most trouble was over his left eye. All another boxer had to do was look at that place over his eye and Charlie would start bleeding.

It was embarrassing to me as both his trainer and brother.

We didn't have a cut man so that was my job too along with everything else.

I would hold a gauze pad to the cut and tell him to stop bleeding already. We would talk strategy as I would hold the gauze pad over his eye and Charlie was usually gasping for air because he was never in good shape despite all that training we did. Maybe the other boxer had a vicious overhand right and I would tell Charlie he had to look out for it. I'd tell him to stay out of the corners and keep to the middle of the ring. I'd tell him if he made it out of the next round alive it would be a miracle.

Then I would smear Vaseline on the cut because that's what professional cut men do.

Then I would tell Charlie to go out there and keep his left up.

Should the phone ring I will say to the caller are you wearing a uniform. I will ask them if they sweat too much in their uniform and if they sweat too much do they chafe too.

If the answer is words then fine I know words and can talk words but if the answer is the caller hanging up then don't bother calling me again.

Why I sweat too much is they don't have air conditioning in here. I ask the doctors who bring me my powder and uniforms about the air conditioning and they say I shouldn't worry about things like that.

I tell them one less thing right.

Then I tell them this is cruel and unusual. I tell them this is what they do to prisoners of war. I tell them they wouldn't have to bother installing the air conditioner because I could take care of it myself. I tell them I was very handy around the house which is a lie but what do they know about it. I tell them Mother made me go out and get a job installing air conditioners because she was unemployed half the time. I tell them all they have to do is buy one for Christ's sake and bring it in here.

Sometimes Charlie and I would pretend to be a military policeman and a foreign prisoner of war. What would happen is I'd be the MP and Charlie would be a foreign agent trying to spy on Alaska. So I'd catch him and throw him up against a wall and frisk him and tell him he had the right to remain silent and that anything he said could be used against him in a court of law with a trial by hung jury. Then after frisking him I'd put the handcuffs on and take him to the cooler which was Mother's bedroom in this particular case.

We made the handcuffs from two of Mother's bracelets but she never found out about it so that too was one less thing.

Should the phone ring Mother would be embarrassed by how I conducted myself over the phone.

What would happen is the phone would ring and back then I didn't say the hello how are you at all. What I said was hello and after the caller said hello back I'd say what do you want.

When Mother heard me say this she said what the fuck is wrong with you. She said you don't speak on the phone that way.

I said I think I do and she said you say the hello how are you who may I ask is calling can I take a message please.

Mother said who taught you to be rude like this over the phone.
I said no one did Mother.
She said are you rude like this in school.
I said I don't think so.
She said from now on you are polite to anyone who calls here on the phone or anyone who speaks to you at all and don't ever let me find out otherwise.

Should the phone ring and it's Mother on the other end I am always polite these days.

Yes I am wearing a uniform is both polite and an act of kindness.

A caller calling on the phone and talking words I understand and not hanging up is an act of kindness.

How a caller can do this is to say one word at a time very slowly. So if they want to ask how I am feeling they should say how and then wait a minute or two so I can think about the word how. How is what the Indians on TV would say to each other as a way of saying hello. They would ride up on their horses and then raise their right arm in the air like someone swearing to tell the truth the whole truth and nothing but the truth so help them God does when they take the stand in a trial by jury. An Indian would never say the hello how are you because for him hello and how mean the same thing. Indians aren't stupid like that because they're Indians. This is something Mother would say to us because whenever Charlie and I would see an Indian on TV we'd always turn to each other and say How and then one or the other of us would say he smoke'm peace pipe how. She would tell us not to make fun of the Indians which isn't what we were doing I don't think. This is when she said Indians aren't stupid like that because they're Indians. She also said that Indians couldn't help being Indians themselves and we shouldn't blame them for it.

Sometimes Charlie and I didn't understand Mother so we didn't know what she wanted us to do half the time. We would look at the floor and nod up and down until she was finished talking.

Charlie and I never pretended to be Indians the way we pretended to be boxers which is something Mother wouldn't have wanted us doing had she known about it. So I would need enough time to think about all this before the caller moved on to the next word in how are you feeling. Then I would need a few minutes to think about are which would make me think of the letter R and how Mother would make us read all the R words in the dictionary and then test us on them. That's all the time I'd need with are which is why it would be hard for callers to know how much time to give me for each word. Some words you need more time with than others.

So yes I am wearing a uniform is an act of kindness the same as a caller talking words so I can understand them. These are two things Charlie would do if he had the sense to do them.

Calling someone on the phone can be an act of kindness but it rarely happens that way. Most calls are cruel and unusual like the callers who say the hello how are you and then go right into who they're cutting or when they try to sell you something you don't need like a newspaper.

Why do callers think I would want to read a newspaper every day because what's in a newspaper that has anything to do with me here.

The trouble with Charlie is he hasn't been the same since the boxing. I think all that boxing turned him into a cruel and unusual person.

The last time I saw Charlie he spoke like he had been given too many pills. I never saw Mother give Charlie his pills so I don't know if she made pill circle or squares for him every day. I don't know if she kissed his forehead or tucked him in goodnight the same way either.

Charlie's bedroom was on the other side of the house so I don't know what went on over there other than when we used to box together.

The last time I saw Charlie his hands were shaking and he couldn't keep his head still.

I remember when we all took Charlie to the doctor that one summer. This was before his hands started shaking or his not being able to keep his head still but it was probably the start of it all.

What happened was we found this boxer Charlie could spar with on one of our morning jogs. I saw him pummeling a football player at the field we always jogged past and thought we should go talk to him.

So we had this fellow come over twice a week to spar with Charlie in Mother's room and everything was fine for a while.

I would have Charlie start off with some jabs and combinations and I would tell him to watch his footwork. The trouble is Charlie would sometimes forget he was supposed to fight right handed and switch his stance to southpaw.

Charlie was born left handed but you can't expect to box and be left handed at the same time so we trained Charlie to box as a righty or what we call conventional in the business.

Too many times Charlie would look down at his feet and this fellow would catch Charlie with a vicious uppercut and so we had to take Charlie to the doctor.

The doctor wired Charlie's jaw shut for him and he had to stay like that for a month.

So there was Charlie with his jaw wired shut and he had to drink all of his food through a straw like an idiot.

This is when we'd go to the ice cream truck every day because Charlie couldn't eat Mother's sandwiches and coleslaw. Mother tried to put the coleslaw in a blender for him but what happened was Charlie didn't like coleslaw that way.

Mother would tell him I don't need this kind of aggravation.

She would tell me the same thing whenever I needed powder for the chafed parts.

Whenever I needed powder for the chafed parts Mother would bring it to me in my room like she did with my pills. Sometimes she would put it on herself but when I got older she let me do it.

That's because I was getting too old for Mother to be poking around down there.

Always Mother had me hold my situation so she could get to the chafed parts. She would say hold your situation so I can get to the chafed parts like that.

Once part of my situation slipped from my hold and Mother said I don't need this kind of aggravation.

The next time it happened she said no one wants to see that.

I didn't forget about the you in how are you but when I think too much about one word and then another I sometimes decide I've had enough of the words and will listen only to the voice from then on. The words aren't as important as the voice and when you listen only to the voice you don't have to think about the words themselves. You can listen to what comes between the words and behind them.

Should the phone ring there will be a caller on the other end though it probably won't be Charlie. Sometimes I ask the callers why they aren't Charlie. I'll say why aren't you Charlie like that and this is when they usually hang up.

It is probably not anyone's fault that they are not Charlie.

What bothers me is they never apologize for intruding and they never apologize for not being Charlie. And none of them ever try pretending to be Charlie. How one of them could do this is to sound cruel and unusual by talking all slowly and mumbly.

I can pretend several accents in several registers myself but what I can't do is actually become the person I am pretending to be the way an actor like Charlie Robertson does. This is because I've no idea who it is I'm pretending to be. I don't know the good or the bad or what that person eats for breakfast every day. This is one reason I am not a professional actor and why callers usually hang up before it goes too far. Some of them get upset with me but who made the mistake in the first place is what I have to say.

Actors are killers just as cigarettes are killers just as drugs are killers just as drunk drivers are killers just as doctors are killers. Doctors are probably the worst killers of all these different kinds of killers.

Charlie would say the same thing if he was here right now. That Charlie isn't here right now is his own fault but I am not angry with him about that. I remember Mother telling me not to be angry with Charlie because he can't help being the way he is. I wanted to ask Mother if I could help being the way I was or if she could help either but I decided against it. Mother didn't like it when you asked her too many questions.

She would say I am not on trial here whenever we asked her questions.

Charlie probably doesn't know that I am the only one here and the only one that has ever been here.

Charlie doesn't know about here.

Here the four walls are painted white and everything else is blue. The bed in here is blue and so are the table and chairs. The blankets are also blue and what's good is it's the same shade of blue as some of my pills.

Here there is a bathroom on the other side of the mirror.

What happens is I have to knock on the mirror whenever I have to use the bathroom which is quite a lot.

I have always had to use the bathroom quite a lot and this always worried Mother especially. She would hear me in the bathroom and ask if I was okay in there. She would say are you okay in there like that and I would say this isn't a good time Mother.

Why I can do several accents in several registers is because I have the ear for it. Mother would tell all kinds of people I had a great ear. She said it was a gift. All the people would look at me and smile and say I was so gifted and then Mother would have me perform for the people. I would do something like pretend to be Joseph Goebbels having his way with Mamie Eisenhower and the people would laugh. Then I would dance a jig because I was a good dancer too

Mother said. Then Mother would clap for me and say to everyone doesn't he have a great ear.

I remember not knowing what she meant when she told people this. I didn't know which ear was great and which one wasn't. I would stare into the bathroom mirror for hours until Charlie pounded on the door and ordered me out.

This is another thing Charlie and I did when we were kids. I'd pretend to be an SS officer and he would be my prisoner because Charlie liked the way I could say we have vays of making you talk.

An SS officer is not the same as an MP or security guard but it was close enough for Charlie.

Mother taught Charlie and I how to dance jigs all over the living room floor one summer. Every night when she'd get home from work we'd dance jigs like this. I was always the best dancer which made both Charlie and Mother jealous.

Should the phone ring there will be someone on the other end talking words. It is often words on the other end though the voices change. It is easier when I know the words when I can say the hello how are you and they ask the same right back. I'm fine I have a headache I didn't sleep last night are all good answers and I try to alternate between those three.

Sometimes I will admit to something else but only if the person on the other end wants to hear it. Almost no one wants to hear it which is why I almost never admit to something else.

Last night the phone rang and it was words on the other end.

I went first and I said the hello how are you like I always do.
I'm fine today and how are you is what came back.
I have a headache I didn't sleep last night is what I said to that.
I'm sorry to hear that Johnny is what the caller said to me next.
This is when I said what did you say to me.
I'm sorry to hear you aren't feeling well today Johnny.
Why are you calling me Johnny.
Why shouldn't I call you Johnny Johnny.
This is when I said who the fuck is Johnny Johnny.
What did we say about swearing Johnny.
We didn't say anything about swearing Johnny.
We most certainly did Johnny.
I don't think we did Johnny because I don't think we've ever spoken before Johnny.
I'm disappointed to hear you say that Johnny.

This is when I hung up in their faces.

I don't know who this caller was or why they called me in the first place or why they kept calling me Johnny. I think it was a wrong number but it almost always is a wrong number when the phone rings.

After a minute or two I decided to concentrate on the voice and leave the words alone. It is always better to listen to the voice instead of the words.

I didn't recognize the voice which is why I think it was a wrong number. Maybe the voice sounded a little like Mother's but only because I think the voice belonged to a woman. The voice sounded like a soprano singing an aria to me. I always like to talk to women because women have nicer voices especially if they are sopranos.

What I never do is pretend some other woman is Mother though.

I don't think it was Mother last night either. I haven't seen Mother for so long now and I don't think she knows I'm here.

Sometimes people call here looking for Charlie. They don't know that Charlie has never been here and that I'm the only one who ever has.

Another thing about here that is cruel and unusual is they won't let me have a television to watch.

I've decided not to ask about a television yet because I'm waiting for them to bring me an air conditioner first. Once they bring me an air conditioner then it's time to talk about a television.

We always had that one television in the living room growing up. The television itself had rabbit ear antennas and was black and white instead of color. I would tell Charlie that we were the only people in the world that still had a black and white television and he would say you know Mother as well as me and of course he was right.

Charlie and I would sometimes fight about what we wanted to watch but because he was older and responsible it was always his decision.

This is when I asked Mother if I could have my own television.

Charlie decided we should watch yet another boxing match and by this time I was sick of the boxing. I told him I would tell Mother what he did to her bracelets unless he changed the channel. When that didn't work I told Charlie he was no good as a boxer and he should take up baseball instead. I told him I wouldn't train him anymore and what was he going to do without a trainer.

Mother was making us sandwiches and coleslaw in the kitchen while we were in the living room so I thought it was a good time to ask.

The living room had the sofa where we would all sit down to watch the television and the television itself. There was a stand for the television and two fake plants on either side of it. Mother couldn't keep real plants alive and she could never count on us to help her either.

Once she gave us hell for allowing one of the real plants to die. She had told us it was our responsibility to water the plant and move it in and out of the sunlight. The trouble is we forgot to do this and Mother came home to find the plant dead and us on the sofa watching television like nothing happened.

She said what did I say to you two.
She said I come home from working all day like a dog and this is what I find.
She said I find the plant dead and you two on the sofa watching television like nothing happened.

She said I told you you were responsible.

She was swinging her ladle around while she said this. This was something Mother liked to do a lot. She loved that ladle and loved to swing it around when she yelled at us.

She kept the ladle hanging in the kitchen so it was never far away.

Whenever Mother yelled at us Charlie and I agreed with her by turning off the television and sitting back down on the sofa.

She punished us that night by having us read two hundred pages of the dictionary each and thank God she forgot to test us by the time we finished.

This is when I told Mother I might try to rewrite the dictionary when I get a chance.

There are a lot of words in there I don't like the definitions for is what I told her.

The kitchen itself was next to the living room but you could only see the television from the kitchen if you were at the table. The rest of the kitchen had a wall that made it impossible to see the television from anywhere inside it.

This is where the sink and counter was and this is where Mother would make us our sandwiches and coleslaw.

So I asked her about buying me my own television because Charlie would never let me watch what I wanted and she told me it was almost time for dinner and we would discuss it tomorrow instead.

I was about to say I don't even care if it's a black and white but this was Mother's way of saying I don't need this kind of aggravation so why bother.

Another truth is people have always confused me with Charlie and vice versa. Some people even said we looked like twins which we certainly weren't. Charlie was older and always responsible. That's how you could tell us apart.

Also Charlie was allowed to get hurt because he wouldn't die from it.

And I was always the better dancer.

I have never liked it when people confuse me with Charlie but I don't blame them for it either. You cannot blame people for what's wrong with them. People can't help it. If Mother taught me anything this is what she taught me. People can't help being people the same way dogs can't help being dogs.

Mother also taught us about singing because she liked it when we would sing during the commercials for her. She taught us all the parts like soprano alto tenor baritone and bass. She would play opera records for us and say this one is a soprano and that one is the great tenor Caruso. She wanted me to learn how to sing an aria like Caruso.

She said that I could make it in show business if I applied myself and I had to otherwise we'd wind up on the streets together.

We only had our dog for one summer because Charlie and Mother didn't like him. Mother brought home the dog one day after work but she didn't say where he came from. She told us not to get attached to the dog because we weren't keeping him. She said the dog was temporary like unemployment.

Why Mother said it this way is because she sometimes was unemployed herself. This wasn't Mother's fault she told us. She said she was a good employee and that her bosses were all cruel and unusual. She said they wanted her to do things that weren't in the job description. We never asked her what those things were and we never asked her to describe her jobs for us either.

She told us she would show up for work on time every day and was early more often than not. She said she would stay late whenever it was necessary even though she never collected overtime. She said she got along well with her co-workers and that everyone liked her. She would tell us this over dinner and we agreed with her by eating all of our dinners and not interrupting.

Charlie would sit to Mother's right and me to her left. Mother said we had to be separated because we would misbehave otherwise. I don't think we ever misbehaved at the dinner table but that didn't matter apparently. I think she was this way because she caught us in Charlie's room with her stoles all stapled together.

At the table Mother would say things like I'm glad that tomorrow is Wednesday so that the next day is Thursday.

Or she'd say I cooked so now the two of you clean.

We would tell her we wanted to watch television instead and she would say I worked all day long and what's your excuse.

We think Mother worked in an office but we never knew for sure.

Charlie and I would do the dishes every night after dinner while Mother took a shower or went into the living room to lie down on the sofa. How we did the dishes was I would wash all the dishes and place them on the dish rack while Charlie stood next to me and did nothing.

Mother wasn't to be disturbed when she was lying on the sofa. On her way to the sofa Mother would say I am not to be disturbed like that.

What she'd do is take off her shoes and put her feet up on the arm of the sofa. Her head would be on a pillow and she'd cover her eyes with her left arm. She liked it dark and quiet so the lights and the television were always off whenever she was laying down.

After the dishes Charlie and I had to go into our own rooms and wait for Mother to say it was okay for us to come out again.

This is when we'd discuss the events of the day. All three of us would sit on the sofa with Mother in the middle.

Mother would say something like tell me about your day.
I would say Charlie you go first.

Charlie would say something like it was another day at school Mother.
Mother would say what did you learn today Charlie.
Charlie would say today we did fractions in math and we memorized the states in civics.

This is when Mother would say Jesus to herself and get up to go to the kitchen. She'd come back with a glass of Scotch whiskey in one hand and a cigarette burning between her lips.

Then she'd look at me and say what about you.
I'd say today it was baseball in gym class.
Then she'd say what about the school part.
I'd say today it was manifest destiny and how they pushed the Indians around.

This is when Mother would get up shaking her head. She would mutter something to herself and then say I'm going to bed I have to get up early for work tomorrow.

I didn't tell her that I didn't understand what manifest had to do with destiny because you know Mother.

I applied for a job one summer but Mother didn't let me go for the interview. She said I was too young to work which meant she was afraid I'd get hurt and die.

I don't know how you can get hurt and die working in an ice cream truck but that was Mother for you.

I think I would like the job of carving the letter P into blue pills. I think I could do this all day long and not get bored. I think I could do this the same way Mother worked like a dog for us except I wouldn't get myself fired like she did all the time. I think I would show up early and stay late whenever there were extra pills to carve. I would get along with all my co-workers and I wouldn't care about overtime either.

I would carve each P the same way for years and then when no one was looking I would carve other letters into the pills like A and C which in this case would stand for air conditioning.

I would spell out what happened to the air conditioning in blue pills like that.

Along with no air conditioning here and no television they won't let me have a clock for the wall either. So on top of everything I never know what time it is.

I can only assume it's morning when they bring me my morning pills and it's time for bed when they bring me the nighttime pills.

I don't know the days of the week either so I could never say something like I'm glad tomorrow is Wednesday so that the next day is Thursday.

Should the phone ring right now I might say can you at least give me the fucking time of day here.

Mother didn't let us name the dog. I wanted to ask her why she brought him home in the first place but this was Mother we're talking about.

That one summer we had the dog was glorious. I would hold the rope around Charlie's back with my left hand and the dog's leash with my right. Sometimes I was afraid the dog wouldn't be able to keep up but that dog was as good a jogger as Charlie and me.

I secretly gave a name to the dog but I've forgotten what it was. No one knew about the name because I think I would've caught hell otherwise.

What I do remember is that the dog's name was not Charlie. It would've been fun to call him Charlie but Charlie himself wouldn't have liked it at all.

I slept with the dog every night that summer. What I'd do is leave him in the living room when Mother came in to give me my pills. Sometimes she would bring me powder for the chafed parts but only during the summer when it was hot and I would sweat too much. But always she gave me my pills every night and after I would make the circle or square disappear I'd pretend to fall asleep right away this way Mother wouldn't be suspicious. Sometimes she would stay with me until I fell asleep. She would sit on the bed and wait. I always felt that if I didn't fall asleep right away I'd be in trouble and this is why I always pretended to fall asleep right away even when we didn't have the dog.

How I would do this is keep my eyes shut and be still for a few minutes and then I would twitch once or twice. Mother would usually get up and leave after the first twitch but sometimes it took two twitches for her to go. The summer we had the dog I'd wait until everyone was asleep and then I'd go into the living room to bring the dog into bed with me. Mother wouldn't have liked it had she known I was sleeping with the dog but who brought him home in the first place.

I don't know whatever happened to the dog. When the summer was over he was gone and I knew better than to ask Mother about it.

Should the phone ring I will not pretend to be Charlie. I never pretend to be Charlie. Charlie wouldn't like it and I would never do that to Charlie.

Whoever it was that called last night and confused me with Charlie didn't apologize for intruding either. This caller was either confused or mistaken or was playing a game with me. Sometimes people like to play games with me to see how I am doing. There are all kinds of games to play to see how I am doing. Sometimes after the game they will tell me I am doing fine. This is when I say I am fine I have a headache I didn't sleep last night. I almost never admit to anything else with these people.

MPs and security guards almost never admit to anything which is why I don't like to either.

I don't mind playing games because Charlie and I would play games together when we were kids. As long as I couldn't get hurt Mother liked it when we played games together. Mother would be in the kitchen cooking us dinner and Charlie and I would be in the living room playing some game or another. We would play board games and card games mostly but I forget which ones. The dog was always trying to horn in on the game but Charlie would smack him across the nose and curse him. There was nothing I could do to stop Charlie from doing this. This is one of the reasons Charlie was such a good boxer because Charlie himself was heartless.

Charlie never let me win because I was the younger brother which was supposed to make me tough. He told me no one in the real world was going to let me win because I was Charlie's younger brother so why should he.

No one ever plays a game where they get to call me Charlie though. This is why I think it was a wrong number or the caller was mistaken.

This is why it is better to say nothing so that when someone calls you Charlie you say nothing back to them. Instead of asking who is Charlie or if they are Charlie themselves you say nothing instead. This will make the caller uneasy and will make the caller want to hang up the phone in their own faces.

I could say to them that I am not Charlie and have not heard from Charlie since he quit boxing but why bother.

Should the phone ring I will say nothing and listen to that nothing coming back through the telephone. It is always better to say nothing and listen to that nothing coming back through the telephone than it is to talk to morons on the other end who mistake you for Charlie.

I have many times held the phone to my ear and listened to the nothing coming through. The nothing coming through the telephone is the best nothing there is. It is almost the epitome of nothing almost the point of absolute nothing. The nothing coming through the telephone is better than the nothing one often finds oneself doing at any particular time and this is always the case.

Someone asks you what are you doing and you say nothing.

I am almost always doing nothing it seems. It hasn't always been like this but it has been like this for as long as I can remember.

Charlie is always doing nothing whenever I talk to him on the telephone. I will call him up and ask what are you doing Charlie and he will say nothing like that. This is not another reason I feel sorry for Charlie because Charlie has always liked doing nothing.

But doing nothing is nothing at all like the nothing coming through the telephone. The nothing through the telephone is ripe it is pregnant it is nuanced. I can listen to this nothing all day long. Anyone can do this but only MPs and security guards can do this for hours on end without getting bored. This is why I think I may've once been an MP or security guard. Boxing trainers could never do this. They are always jumping up and down outside the ropes in their corners and yelling and screaming at both Charlie and the referee.

Charlie could listen to the nothing for hours too. Two whole summers we sat in the living room and listened to the nothing. We'd get up while it was still dark out and go into the living room without eating breakfast or brushing our teeth. We'd sit on opposite ends of the sofa and listen to the nothing until we were finished. I knew we were finished when Charlie got up to go to the bathroom. Then we could have our breakfast and do what we'd want as long as I couldn't get hurt from it.

Charlie called listening to the nothing meditating. I didn't know that was what we were doing together in the living room. Before we meditated together in the living room Charlie would go off into this room to meditate by himself. He would say this he would say I am going to my room to meditate. We would be in the living room watching television when he would all of a sudden say this. This is when he would get up and walk to his room closing the door behind him. He would be in there for up to half an hour sometimes.

I would go to the door and listen. I would press a glass to the door and stick my great ear inside the glass because I saw someone do this in a movie once. It never worked for me though. I could never hear Charlie meditating there in his room.

At the time I thought meditating was the same as masturbating.

I thought it was another word for masturbating.

Why I thought it was another word was Charlie taught me the word masturbating the summer we had the dog.

The dog would try to hump the two of us and when Mother saw the dog doing this she would get angry and curse him. She would say stop it you goddamned dog and then Charlie would smack it across the nose and the dog would stop.

I asked Charlie why the dog did this to us and this is when

he taught me the word masturbating.

Charlie said the dog humping us was how he masturbated. He said the dog couldn't masturbate otherwise so he humps his owners instead. I asked Charlie why a dog would want to masturbate in the first place and he said it was human nature. This is when I asked him if he masturbated himself and what Charlie did was smack me across the nose.

I said what did you do that for Charlie.
Charlie said you don't ask someone if they masturbate themselves.
I said why not.
Charlie said that masturbation is private and you only do it in your room by yourself.
I said like you do all the time.
Charlie said I am in my room meditating all the time.
I said how do you do it then.
Charlie said how do you meditate.
I said no masturbate.
He said you go into your room and then do what feels good. He said boxers when they are training aren't supposed to masturbate anyway and that he would never do such a thing. Then I asked him if masturbating had anything to do with meditating.
Charlie said no they have nothing to do with each other.
I asked him why do people meditate then.
Charlie said people meditate to be at one with themselves. He said the best boxers in the world meditate because it helps them with their boxing. This is why we have to meditate every day is how Charlie finished the conversation.

There is no one way to listen to the nothing. It is only important that you too say nothing this way the nothing

goes uninterrupted. To interrupt the nothing is a bad idea.
I learned all this from Charlie.

The first few times we meditated together I interrupted to
ask if I was doing it right. I didn't know how to meditate
myself and wasn't allowed to look at Charlie doing it.
Charlie said we had to keep our eyes closed during the
meditation otherwise it wouldn't work. So the first few times
I interrupted Charlie meditating was when he'd smack me
and tell me to listen to the nothing and breathe.

That summer Charlie told me that for ages there was only
the nothing and nothing else. In the beginning there was
nothing and it was good. It was good like this a long time
until the nothing was interrupted by the advent of animals
and people.

What we think of the beginning was not the actual beginning
Charlie said. We think of the beginning as the beginning
of heaven and earth and the earth without form and void
and darkness upon the face of the deep and then the light
that was good and dividing the light from the darkness and
then calling the light Day and the darkness Night. Then the
firmament in the midst of the waters and this firmament
became heaven and then came dry land Earth and this was
good and then grass and seed and the fruit tree and lights
from the firmament and all this happened by the fourth day
and still there was still the nothing that was there before.
Maybe it wasn't the same exact nothing as before but it was
in the same family of nothing and very similar to what we
recognize as the nothing of today. This all changed when
the waters that brought forth the moving creature that hath

life and once you have moving creatures that hath life you interrupt the nothing. Then the fowl that may fly above the earth in the open firmament of heaven which interrupted the nothing even more and all of this would've been fine had it not been for what came next. What came next was that they were to be fruitful and multiply and fill the waters of the seas and the earth and the sky forever drowning out the nothing that was there before. And still this would've been fine had it not been for the cattle and creeping thing and all beasts of the earth after their kind. All of this was supposed to be good but maybe some of it wasn't. And we can only know if something is good if we have something either bad or not quite as good to compare it to and before this there was only the nothing which went unrecognized and because of this was not considered either good or not good. Then man after the likeness and dominion over the fish of the sea and fowl of the air and over cattle and every creeping thing that creepeth upon the earth and then go fruitful and multiply and the nothing gone forever. Only here and there do we catch even a speck of the nothing and never as before the beginning of heaven and earth.

Charlie would tell me about this over and over and he would finish by saying pay heed to this my friend lest you draw his ire.

Mother called him a fanatic and me his accomplice.

This was one of those times when I didn't know what one word had to do with another.

This is why I have trouble when people say good morning or good evening. I don't understand why people use good morning or good evening to say the hello how are you instead

of saying the hello how are you like everyone else.
So according to Charlie there was a beginning before the beginning and it was the nothing.

Charlie said this is another reason we meditate. We meditate to return to the nothing where we once belonged. He said that was God's plan.

The nothing lasted forever up to the point of the beginning. Forever is forever and cannot be measured in time Charlie said. Five minutes of forever is the same as eons.

For instance the nothing that came through the telephone last night lasted forever.

When you don't know the days of the week you don't know what month it is either and when you don't know what month it is you don't know when it's time to celebrate your birthday.

I don't know how many birthdays I've missed in here. What I do know is no one ever comes in here and says happy birthday to me. No one brings me a happy birthday cake with candles in it and sings the happy birthday song either. No one ever brings me a birthday gift which is why they sometimes remind me so much of Mother.

Sometimes if I'm doing especially well on the tests they bring me ice cream in a cardboard cup. The ice cream cup has a top with a lip to peel off if you want to eat the ice cream before it melts. The first time they brought it to me here I wasn't sure how to peel that lip off and this is what happened.

Whenever they bring me the ice cream I ask them is it my birthday today and what they say to that is how would we know Johnny.

This is when I tell them unless they bring me an air conditioner television and calendar I'm afraid I won't be able to help them much longer.

Then I say who the fuck is Johnny.

Should the phone ring I will say the hello how are you and listen to the words that come back. Sometimes the nothing comes back and it is good. When the nothing comes back I am only too happy to hear it. I listen to the nothing and am grateful there aren't words.

I could go the rest of my life without words and be fine.

The nothing through the telephone isn't the same as meditating. Even though I have plenty of time to do it I don't meditate anymore. It's not the same meditating without Charlie next to me on the living room couch.

Should the phone ring and it's nothing is when it might be Charlie on the other end. Only Charlie would hear the nothing and not interrupt it. I never interrupt it either. Even if I want to say is that you Charlie I don't.

I remember one time after we meditated together I asked Charlie about death about what happens to you when you die. I asked him if it was the same as nothing. Charlie said he didn't think it was nothing but also that he didn't like to think about it either. He said he would wake up screaming in the middle of the night because he dreamed he was dead. Charlie said he would wake up sweating and his heart would stop short and he'd find himself trying to crawl out the window. He said he couldn't breathe when he thought he was dead like this. I asked Charlie what was wrong with him and he said he didn't know. He made me promise not to tell Mother which I never did.

Charlie was afraid of what Mother would do to him is what I think.

Charlie said that death was either something or nothing and if it was nothing then there was nothing to fear because you shouldn't fear nothing and if it is something then it is just as likely to be something good as something bad. This is when I asked Charlie if that is like heaven and hell and he answered by going into his room and closing the door.

I never heard Charlie scream in the middle of the night which is why I think he was lying to me when he said that.

Charlie's room was on the other side of the house but I think I would've heard him screaming regardless.

The people who play games with me do it to see how I am doing. Sometimes they tell me I am doing fine and I tell them so are they.

What happens is the doctors in the white coats and clipboards come in and sit down next to me. They tell me we are going to examine you and I say why bother. Then one of them holds a pen with a light up and tells me to keep my eye on it as he moves it back and forth. Another one takes a hammer out and beats my knees with it. Then the first one has me rearrange shapes into a puzzle the way it is supposed to go. What he'll do is show me first and then I am supposed to do it the same exact way. The puzzle has circles and squares and different slots for them to fit into. This is when I tell them about Mother's pill circles and how that I always made them disappear and they tell me I should concentrate instead.

This is what they like to do with me here.

This is why they remind me of Mother and Charlie sometimes.

Here is a room with four walls and one window and almost nothing else. Yes I have a table and chairs but there is no television or air conditioner here. Yes I have a phone and it does ring sometimes but whose doesn't is what I have to say.

What I do sometimes is measure the room. How I do this is I lay down on the floor with my feet against the back wall. Then I mark in chalk where the top of my head is and I get up and lay down again and this time I put my feet where the chalk mark is. I can do this two and half times before I run out of room.

So the room is two and a half by two and a half which means I think it's a perfect square.

They let me have colored chalk in here and this is the kind of thing Mother would say I was lucky to have. She would say you don't know how lucky you are and I would tell her you're right I don't.

Should the phone ring it might be the person who called last night. I don't know this person but they acted otherwise with me. Why I think this is because right after I said the hello how are you this person told me a story and didn't stop until they were finished.

This wasn't the same one who mistook me for Charlie because not everyone does that. Sometimes people tell me stories like they are testing me. Sometimes these people are doctors and after the test I tell them the answer and they tell me I'm doing fine. These stories are like the riddles I would have Charlie answer though he never did.

It starts with the hello how are you and then the person on the other end who was probably a doctor says a man in a three-piece suit is on the beach and lying face down on a checkered blanket.

So I say okay there is a man a three-piece suit a beach and a checkered blanket.

The doctor says that's right and he has a towel draped over his head and is barefoot. There is a flesh colored band-aid affixed to the back of his left hand and it has been there for days. He cannot remember if he had applied the band-aid himself or if someone had done it for him.

I say good because I remember Mother applying the same kind of band-aid for me when I would cut myself open like the time I fell off the skateboard and hurt my knee. Charlie was pulling me along with the rope we'd tied around his waist and I had one hand holding that rope and the other holding the dog's leash. Everything was fine for a while and we were expecting to be done soon so I could give Charlie his breakfast of raw eggs and milk. Then Charlie must've forgotten he was pulling us along because he stopped short and what happened was the dog and I ran right into him and everyone crashed into each other and all over the street.

I said what the fuck did you stop short for Charlie.
I don't remember what Charlie said to that.
Then I said now we have to go home and who knows what Mother will say.

So all three of us limped home and my knee was bleeding and that's when Mother applied the band-aid for me.

First she asked us what we were doing out so early and we answered by keeping our heads down and bleeding all over the floor.

She said we weren't allowed to leave the house until further notice. She said to Charlie you are supposed to be the responsible one. She was beating him with a ladle when she said this.

Mother always had the ladle hanging up in the kitchen so it was never far away.

Mother didn't like it when she would beat Charlie with the ladle though.

She would say to him why do you make me do this to you.

Then the doctor says next to him on the blanket is a cooler

filled with root beer and turkey sandwiches. There might also be an apple inside the cooler but the apple isn't important.

So I say to the doctor the apple is a trick question.

The doctor says not exactly but it's close.

I say please continue.

The doctor says next to the cooler is a naked woman. The woman is lying on her back and is using her left arm to shade her eyes. There are other men and women and children lying on blankets and sitting on chairs and playing in the sand. Some are splashing in the water others are tossing Frisbees at each other or flying kites.

This is when I think about the dog and how he could never catch a Frisbee himself. Charlie and I would take him out to the backyard and throw the Frisbee around but he could never catch it. What he'd do instead is chase after it and then decide why bother.

So because I think about the word Frisbee I'm not sure if I've missed part of the riddle.

Next I hear the doctor say these other people are wearing a variety of swimsuits and other beachwear. The day is glorious. The sky is blue and cloudless and has the big yellow sun right in the middle of it. The ocean is a mixture of foamy blues and greens. Maybe two hundred feet off shore dolphins are playing and teenagers on jet skis speed after them bouncing on the waves. The dolphins leap out of the water and twist in the air and when they do the people on the beach hoop and holler. Some take pictures and others mostly children imitate the dolphins' movements.

I say to the doctor this is a long riddle.

The doctor says you have to pay attention it's almost over.
Then he says now the man and the woman are not paying attention to the dolphins either.
I say who can blame them at this point.
The doctor says in his head the man is compiling a list of death euphemisms. So far he has passed away passed on expired bought the farm checked out cashed in headed for the happy hunting ground six feet under down for the dirt nap pushing up daisies. When he's finished he will move on to related circumlocutions starting with being under the weather and better the devil.
I say what the fuck kind of word is circumlocution.
The doctor says what did we say about the swearing.
I say I forgot.
The doctor says the other people walk to the water's edge for a closer look. They are careful not to disturb the man in his suit or the naked woman. They ask themselves and each other questions about the man and woman as they walk by them. They do this while keeping an eye out for the dolphins. This is when the woman flips over to sun the other side of herself. The backside is a shade lighter than the front side. The man stays face down on the blanket. Right now he is between one foot in the grave and he who hesitates. There is a collective gasp from the beachgoers as one dolphin executes an impressive midair maneuver and then disappears under the water. Finally the man says to the naked woman basically all I'm guilty of is and it ends with that's what I've been telling you she says before he can finish.

So I answer the man is Charlie the naked woman is Mother and I am the dolphins swimming in the ocean.

This is when the doctor tells me excellent I'm doing fine. Except that Charlie and I never saw Mother naked and we never tried to either.

The naked woman was supposed to distract me from the answer I think. I think the doctor wanted me to think about the naked woman so I would want to be alone with myself instead of answering.

Mother never wanted us to see a naked woman herself. Whenever we would watch a movie together and it looked like the woman was about to be naked Mother would change the channel instead.

Sometimes she would turn the television off because of the filth. She would say television is filth and we shouldn't watch it all the time.

This is when Mother would find something nice on the radio for us to listen to. Sometimes it was a talk show and other times opera and always Charlie would get up to go to his room and leave me alone with Mother and the radio.

Should the phone ring what might come back is what radio people call dead air. Dead air is similar to nothing. In fact it is the same thing. Nothing is dead air the same way dead air is nothing.

Charlie and I would listen to Charlie's radio together whenever there wasn't any boxing or movies on. Whenever there was dead air we would look at each other like maybe something happened to Charlie's radio. We thought maybe Charlie's radio was broken. Then the radio people would say something about dead air and go on with the show.

Charlie had a big fancy radio in his room and I had only a small transistor for mine. This is because Charlie bought his radio himself and Mother couldn't afford to get me the same one. I asked her for one that Christmas and she told me she couldn't afford it because she was unemployed again. She said her boss wanted her to work late and she knew what that meant so she got herself fired instead. She said she was sorry and that maybe next year things would be different.

I can't remember if things were different next year but they probably weren't so why bother.

Charlie's radio had a dual cassette player and all kinds of buttons that did fancy things. It even came with a microphone so that we could make recordings. Charlie recorded most of my performances one summer and we gave it to Mother as a Christmas gift even though she probably didn't appreciate it.

I've never been on the radio myself but I've heard radio people talk about dead air plenty of times. Radio people hate dead air the way callers hate it when you pretend to be the person they intended to call.

I would listen to my transistor after Mother gave me my pills and I pretended to fall asleep so she'd go away. I kept it under my bed so she wouldn't find it. I think if I'd kept it under my head pillow she would've found it which is why I didn't keep it there. Why I think this is because of the way she tucked me in goodnight. She would fluff my head pillow for me before I got the chance to lay my head on it. So I kept the transistor under my bed and I listened to baseball games once Mother went away. There was never any boxing on so it was baseball games I had to listen to.

Mother would ask me why I needed so many pillows. She would say why do you need so many pillows like that. I would answer her by falling asleep as quickly as I could.

Radio people are in show business the same as actors. Mother wanted me to go into show business on account of my ear. She said my kind of talent was one in a million and who could argue.

I did try to act once in school but I was horrible at it. The teacher told me this herself. She said you are a horrible actor like that.

The trouble was she made me use my own voice instead of my ear.

This is when Mother sent me for singing lessons instead. I only had two because Mother got herself fired again and couldn't afford it anymore.

The singing teacher had me sing scales up and down and then she taught me vibrato. If my singing teacher taught me anything this is what she taught me.

There is no telling if Charlie Robertson is a good actor or not or if his teacher ever told him he was horrible. There is no telling if he's ever played an MP or security guard on stage even once in his career. That's because he's not real.

Charlie Robertson is not the same as my brother Charlie. How you can tell them apart is Charlie Robertson is the hypothetical actor I made up and Charlie is my real life brother.

I made up the hypothetical actor Charlie Robertson to piss Charlie off.

Charlie likes to think he is the only Charlie in the world.

What separates Charlie from other Charlies is he's left handed which is another reason he was a lousy boxer.

This is why Charlie could never remember to keep his left up because to him his left was his right and vice-versa.

When dead air happens it is important to keep it dead. One shouldn't speak to interrupt dead air. Once air is dead it should stay dead is another way of saying what I'm saying.

There is no saving dead air is another way.

Should the phone ring it might not be an actual person on the other end. It might be a military policeman or security guard. Everybody knows military policemen and security guards are not real people. They don't look real and they don't talk real. They are supposed to stand in their uniforms and look unreal and patrol for intruders. Only unreal people can do this. Only unreal people can become MPs and security guards.

The same goes for actors. Actors are likewise unreal.

Should the phone ring it might be a recording of an actual person. In some ways these people are professional actors playing the part of a salesperson. They pretend to be lifelike. They affect a voice that cannot be real and cannot be the voice they talk around with all day. People recognize this voice at once and when they do they roll their eyes. People sometimes let out a breath as if they've been jabbed in the stomach with a nightstick when they hear this voice.

Even if this voice is someone you know like your mother or brother you still don't want to hear this voice. Even if you know your mother or brother does this for a living and they rely on selling people things over the phone to keep themselves off the street you still don't want to hear this voice.

They use your name with this voice over and over like doctors in white coats do. Most often this person is trying to sell you something for your house. People without houses probably don't receive these calls or if they do they probably get upset when these calls come. These people are doubly bothered by these calls because they are reminded they are too poor to have their own house. They probably say how dare you offer me a free gizmo with my purchase in that ridiculous voice you're affecting at me right now.

This is how Mother would talk to these people on the phone. Mother would tell them how she gave birth to Charlie and me and that it tore her insides out. She'd say the three of us would be on the street soon because she was unemployed and the world was cruel and unusual. She'd say she was a good employee but her bosses wanted her to work overtime so she gets fired instead.

I am the same way when I get these calls. This is how you know Mother did give birth to me the way she said. Charlie used to say we were both adopted but Mother wouldn't adopt anyone she didn't give birth to and we all looked too much like each other to be adopted anyway. Charlie looked like Mother and I looked like Charlie.

Charlie would say this adoption talk to be funny which he almost never was.

I yell into the receiver forgetting there is no one on the other end listening. I yell into the receiver for a good minute or two before I realize this. I tell them I am the only one here and that Charlie has never been here and Mother neither. I tell them that Charlie hasn't been the same since the boxing and that he is a sad case.

Instead of hanging up then I tell them they should call Charlie themselves and see what Charlie has to say for himself. I tell them to give Charlie my regards.

The trouble is I feel like an idiot whenever this happens to me. I don't know why this happens but because it also happened to Mother is why I think it might be normal.

Mother would also get upset like this when she had jury duty.

I remember Mother got called for jury duty and had to miss work for two weeks and this was another time she got herself fired.

I asked Mother why she got called for jury duty.

Mother said she didn't know.
I asked her if it was going to be a hung jury and she had me read the dictionary instead of answering.

This time it was Fs and I memorized frigid and fringe and fritter and frivolous which means beside the point which is what I always told Mother reading the dictionary was like.

This is when I most want to pretend like I am an actor playing a military policeman or security guard because actors who play MPs or security guards never yell into a telephone and feel like idiots. Actors and MPs and security guards know better. They know better because they are better.

If I was better I wouldn't be here.

If I was better I'd be somewhere acting on a stage as an MP or security guard and after the performance everyone would clap and say doesn't he have a great ear.

I always wonder what the person who recorded the message is doing while their recorded voice is trying to sell me something I have no use for and I am yelling and cursing at them.

That is something Mother would say to me and Charlie when she wanted us to set the table or make our beds. She would say why don't you make yourself useful.

I made myself useful when Mother and I visited Charlie in the hospital. This was from when Charlie had his jaw wired shut and couldn't eat solid food. Mother tried to put his coleslaw in the blender but you know Charlie.

Instead Charlie lost twenty-five pounds in two weeks and we had to take him to the hospital. The doctors said he was malnourished and dehydrated. They said he would need intensive care so that's where they put him.

The day we went to visit Charlie in intensive care we asked for Charlie at the front desk and the front desk said we should go into the doctor's office ourselves. When we got in there there were two doctors talking about Charlie's case except they were doing this in Spanish.

I think one of the doctors said someone named Maria Conchita took sandwiches and coleslaw from the hospital. Why I think this is he said the word sangre which I think is Spanish for sandwiches and coleslaw. The doctor who said this was called Doctor Sixto. There was a younger doctor to his right who called him Doctor Sixto whenever they said something to each other. This other doctor was an idiot because he had nothing else to say for himself other than yes Doctor Sixto or no Doctor Sixto.

This is when Mother asked about Charlie. She said where is Charlie and what is wrong with him like that.

Doctor Sixto crossed his legs and the idiot doctor to his right handed him a cigar. Above the two of them on the wall was a picture of a young woman. Her hands were folded under her chin and she was looking down so that you couldn't see her eyes.

This is the kind of picture the doctors here show me and

then ask what I think about it. They want to know who I think the young woman is. They want to know her name how old she is where she lives does she have any brothers and sisters and why she is looking down.

So I say her name is Maria Conchita she is sixteen years old she lives in Alaska she has a brother named Charlie and she is looking down because Mother is yelling at her with a ladle so what do you expect.

At the hospital Doctor Sixto ran the cigar under his nose and this is when Mother said this is too much. I think I said I couldn't agree more but I can't remember. I think Mother gave me too many pills that morning so it's hard to remember.

Otherwise the doctors here gave me too many pills this morning which amounts to the same thing.

Doctor Sixto had a thin gray mustache and was halfway bald and looked like an old bullfighter to me. It looked like he had been alive a long time almost from the advent of animals and people.

So again we told him we needed to find Charlie and that he was malnourished and dehydrated and in intensive care.

Instead of answering us Doctor Sixto said something in Spanish to the idiot doctor. He was holding the cigar in his hand but wasn't smoking it.

By this time Mother said she was going to contact her attorney which was a lie because she didn't have one then.

So we went back to the front desk and this time they told us where Charlie was. We took the elevator up to intensive care and it was real heartbreak once we got up there.

They had Charlie hooked up to three different tubes and a hose running into his mouth so he could breathe easy. Mother said look at what they did to your brother Charlie and I said I know. Mother said this is real heartbreak and I said who can argue.

This is when Mother said why don't you make yourself useful and go down to the cafeteria and get me cigarettes. She handed me a twenty dollar bill and said I should order myself a sandwich.

I rode the elevator down with two security guards and a nurse and I asked them where the cafeteria was and they all told me it was on the first floor to the right.

These security guards were handsome in their uniforms and said it was on the first floor to the right with authority.

What happened next was I ordered myself a sandwich and sat down in the cafeteria next to a woman drinking coffee. There was nowhere else to sit and I didn't want to eat my sandwich standing up so this is what I had to do. I also didn't want to eat it in front of Charlie because of how malnourished he was.

You know how jealous he gets.

I opened my sandwich from the wrapper and the woman next

to me said the doctors can't tell me why my husband died.
I said I'll get Mother for you she's upstairs.
Then she said I think it's because they killed him and don't want me to sue.
I told her Charlie was upstairs in intensive care and had tubes eating and breathing for him. I told her Mother is in his room right now waiting for me to bring her cigarettes.
She said I should've asked questions is what I think.
Then she said the lawyers were pleased to tell me about the house though. They aren't worried about litigation like the doctors. Otherwise they are the exact same people.

I said really but what I wanted to do was take my sandwich and leave. I didn't want to go back up to intensive care but I had nowhere else to go. What I wanted to say to this lady was I'm fine which means please stop talking.

But Mother said I wasn't allowed to be rude so I had no choice.

The woman said the doctors who killed my husband are the lawyers who told me about the house. There are three of them all with the same parts in their hair and the same bifocals.

I told her Charlie has to wear glasses when he reads which was another lie.

This is when she said I think I accused them of moonlighting though sometimes when I remember it I accused them of gaslighting.
I told her I'm not sure there is a difference.
She said they looked at me funny both times which is something I'm used to since my husband died. When they

were lawyers they wanted to hand me papers have me sign the papers and get me out of the office without touching anything. People are like that around a newly widowed widow.
She said it's like you're contagious.
She said you see people holding their breath.

I told her I didn't think Charlie was contagious but you can't be too careful regardless.

She said my husband never told me he owned another house.
I said I bet that isn't the only thing he never told you.

She said you're sweet.
She said you remind me of my nephew.
She said he's dead now too.

I said what's your nephew's name and she answered by saying the house my husband left me isn't what you'd think of when you think of husbands leaving wives houses.
I said what's it like then.
She said at the end of a private dirt road with trees and bushes lining both sides is a musty bungalow. There are two wings to the bungalow on opposite sides of the kitchen. There is no furniture in any of the rooms and no appliances in the kitchen. That first day I examined each room looking for signs of life. Other than a team of spiders and other insects I don't think anyone has ever lived there.
I said it sounds a lot like our house except we have a black and white television in the living room.
She said what happened to Charlie why is he upstairs in intensive care.
I said he forgot to keep his left up again.

She said I've decided not to live in this house.

I said you can stay with us if Mother says it's okay.

She said it didn't take me long to come to this decision. I didn't have to consult anyone and I don't have to answer to anyone either. I did consider burning the house to the ground but I don't know how to go about that sort of thing. I told her if Charlie wakes up he could help you with that if you want.

Then she said I didn't consider this for too long.

She said there's no one I want to give this house to as a gift either.

She said no one I know deserves a house.

This is when I took the last bite of my sandwich and told her I had to go back upstairs to see my brother Charlie in intensive care.

She took a sip of her coffee and didn't look up.

Once I got back upstairs Mother said it was time to leave which we all thanked God for.

I never saw that woman again so I don't know whatever became of her or that house. I didn't tell Mother about the woman either.

Should the phone ring it might be one of the voices trying to sell insurance. They tell you there is no obligation and they offer a free quote. I never ask them what kind of insurance because why bother. I don't think I have insurance and I don't think I need it.

Whenever I hear this kind of call my head cracks open and I

spill out all over the floor.

This is when they have to come in here and clean up after me.

One of them comes in here with a mop and another one with a bucket. I sit on the bed with my feet up so they won't miss a spot and cheer them on.

This is like how when Mother used to vacuum in the living room except she made Charlie and me do it most of the time.

The floor here is cement and easy to clean up after. It's also good for drawing on in chalk.

They let me draw stick figures on the floor so this is what I do all day long.

I draw stick figures in relation to other stick figures. Some stick figures are dancing jigs while others are singing during the commercials. Some are seated at a kitchen table eating sandwiches and coleslaw and others are meditating on the living room sofa.

In one drawing there are two stick figures trying to sneak into a private school with two stick security guards chasing them away. Right next to that one is a stick figure jogging with a rope tied around his waist and he is pulling along another stick figure riding on a skateboard. This stick figure is holding a dog's leash and there is a stick dog jogging along beside them.

There are two stick figures pushing another stick figure in a stick wheelchair on one side of a street while another stick figure harasses two female stick figures on the other.

How this one works is the two stick figures pushing the other stick figure in a stick wheelchair is Mother and I pushing Charlie around in a wheelchair after he got out of the hospital that one time.

There may well be a professional actor named Charlie Robertson. If there is he probably isn't good because I've never heard of him. He may be one of these actors that waits tables all day long instead of acting.

He might take a class or two at night and go on auditions during the day. Or he goes to a small rural town every summer to do what actors call summer stock. Summer stock is another thing actors make up. There is no such thing as summer stock. Actors want people to think they do act sometimes so they tell people this. I'm not sure anyone believes it.

Charlie Robertson is probably one of these kinds of actors if he is an actual actor.

I know about summer stock because Charlie tried to be an actor after he finished boxing. I don't know why he thought he could do this when he couldn't keep his hands and head from shaking but Charlie always knew better.

Charlie made me rehearse with him two whole summers. What we'd do is wake up while it was still dark out and meet in the living room so we could rehearse. Mother would still be sleeping I think. Otherwise she wasn't home yet from her night job. Mother sometimes had to work at night in order to keep us off the streets. Mother said she had to make all kinds of sacrifices because she gave birth to the two of us and she rued the day. She said this is why I had to make it in show business.

I didn't know any of the plays Charlie and I rehearsed together in the living room. Except that Charlie never called them plays he called them scenes.

Charlie came out wearing a bathrobe and sucking on a pretzel stick which was supposed to be a cigar. I had a crutch which was actually my old baseball bat from that one summer they let me play on the team. I was Charlie's son and he was the father. Charlie was supposed to be some kind of famous writer and I was supposed to be his lazy crippled son.

Charlie the father said there you are son.
I said I had plans but maybe after breakfast.
Charlie the father said a man without ambition is a waste of everyone's time.
I said I had ambition daddy.
Charlie the father said I didn't notice anything but then again.
I said I'm not sure but I'll let you know when I do.
Then Charlie the father said you need to exercise your imagination son.
I said I would try after breakfast.
Charlie the father said you are clever like your old man but you are lazy like a gorilla. Had the gorilla any ambition at all he'd be a man today.
I said so what are you are working on daddy.
Prattle Charlie the father said. It is all prattle but they will call it gold.
I said why would they do that daddy.
Because what do they know Charlie the father said.

This is when Charlie the father did what he called his soliloquy. I was allowed to sit on the couch when Charlie did this part of the scene because all I had to do was listen.

Charlie the father said this one involves a few people the way they all involve a few people with some people being more important than other people and the importance of the important people can only be measured against the relative unimportance of the unimportant people which is to say that these people are only unimportant because we have made them that way unimportant we have endowed them with this overarching unimportance our own imaginations failing us and even though some of these unimportant people are smarter and prettier and faster than the important people who let's face it some of the important people are ambitious in ugly ways and they can be greedy and selfish and manipulative in ways that make the unimportant people people we may now call righteous people because they do not behave in this manner and who along with this more agreeable behavior are sometimes smarter and prettier and faster than the important people these unimportant people are dignified and have an integrity that is alien to the important people so these unimportant people we used to think of as unimportant because they lacked a certain something a certain quality call it charisma or gravitas or je ne sais quois or whatever you'd like to call it because perception and reality are entirely distinct from each other and our imaginations are gone from sight these heretofore unimportant people but now altogether righteous people recoil from the ambitious unhealthy important people because why shouldn't they after all these unimportant people have rights too they pay taxes too and then you start to think nothing is this black and white and nothing is this cut and dried and maybe some of the important people aren't always important and some of the unimportant people aren't always unimportant and maybe they do have some things in common or there is some cross-pollination occurring here and one shouldn't point fingers or paint with broad strokes or do anything that can be described in a familiar platitude and perhaps maybe our imaginations aren't all the way dead which makes everything all the more vexing and you think to yourself you think these people are fucked and surely all of this takes place in a place with a climate and a social structure and there are natural elements and unnatural elements and there are familiar markers everywhere you look a house an apartment a street corner and there is food and wine and cigarette smoke and time passes and peace comes to those who wait and time passes again and there is conversation in this place which is a place both peculiar and charming in an oddly familiar yet somehow foreign and exotic way and you have these important people and these unimportant people and the people who exhibit traits from both paradigms who we shall now call the unimportant important people in a place like this place and in a time like this time and they are all of them involved with themselves and with each other and you can never tell by looking at them which is which is which.

The way Charlie did this soliloquy would make your head come off its shoulders. He flailed his arms up and down and spittle flew from his mouth in every direction. He contorted his face and moved his eyebrows up and down without stopping. The trouble was Charlie couldn't keep his hands or his head from shaking so you spent a lot of time watching him shake instead of watching him act but he delivered the speech perfectly each time regardless.

Charlie himself was a great actor I thought if not for all the shaking.

I didn't know what the soliloquy was about and neither did Charlie. I know this because I asked him what the soliloquy was about and he asked me what I thought it was about. When I told him I didn't know he said he didn't either. He said that doesn't mean it wasn't great though.

I asked him how he memorized the entire speech like that and he said it was because he meditated.

Charlie said lots of boxers turn to acting when their careers are over and almost all of them meditate.

It's hard to know if Charlie was a better boxer or actor. As a boxer Charlie had a good jab and a short right that could knock anyone's head off. Charlie's combinations were dangerous which is why no one wanted to stand toe to toe with him. Other boxers would dance around and try to stay away from Charlie for as long as possible. They'd wait for Charlie to get impatient and switch back to southpaw which he almost always did. He was the same way with meditating. He said he should meditate for two hours every day but he never lasted that long. After thirty minutes he'd get up and find something else to do.

So what would happen is Charlie would go on the offensive and leave himself wide open. As his trainer I was outside the ropes yelling and screaming at him to keep his left up but he wouldn't listen. He'd try some combination and the other boxer would counter with a short right of his own and it was crying time again. Charlie would be on the canvas and the referee would count one two three four and I knew Charlie wasn't getting up for the look on his eye. Charlie looked the way he probably looked when he woke up screaming in the middle of the night because he thought he was dead. So the referee counts one two three four and I say please get up Charlie get up Charlie get up but Charlie doesn't listen and the referee reaches ten and I climb inside the ring to wake Charlie up. I smack him his face once or twice and squirt water all over him. This is when Charlie wakes up and I tell him it's okay that he tried his best and that next time he should keep his goddamned left up.

Should the phone ring I might ignore it altogether. If it's Charlie then he'd probably understand and if it isn't Charlie then it's none of my business.

If Charlie kept his left up who knows what would've happened to all of us.

Should the phone ring and it's people on the other end I will say hello people and then I will say you have to have ambition people and that if you were a gorilla would you still be lazy after breakfast like Charlie.

Should the phone ring it might be Charlie on the other end because the last time he called he said he had to go and would call me right back.

Once when Charlie called he said he had several appointments and would be in the area.

I didn't believe him so I said what kind of appointments Charlie. Charlie said he would try to stop by but not that I should wait around for him if I had something to do I should do it and we would catch up with each other later.

I said what the hell are you talking about Charlie. Then I said do you even know the area Charlie.

Charlie said there were some things he wanted to discuss but it wasn't something I should alter my routine over.

This is when I said to myself this isn't the Charlie I know. The Charlie I know is a fanatic and he doesn't talk like this but I thought I should play along anyway.

I said to myself Charlie never should've become a boxer.

So I told Charlie I didn't need to see him but if he needed to see me I would be drawing stick figures on the floor most of the day.

Then Charlie asked if I get bored drawing.

I was about to say I don't know when Charlie said some of his appointments might run long.

Charlie said he had to visit an Indian couple that didn't speak English.

I said he smoke'm peacepipe Charlie.

Charlie said goodbye by saying they always give Indians to the new guys and hanging up.

This is why you never know with Charlie.

You never know what he's going to say or do next but this is always what's made Charlie Charlie especially after the boxing.

It's when people use words they shouldn't is when we get in trouble with ourselves. One caller asked me for an allocution once before I was even finished with the hello how are you and I had to hang up in his face. I didn't know who this caller was and no one had told me to expect a call like this. I probably had to read allocution when I did the As but I can't remember what it means. This is when Mother would say I should make myself useful which meant to leave her the hell alone.

Allocution is a word no one should use over the phone intruders especially.

The caller's voice was deep and gruff and sounded a little like Charlie's. Charlie has had this kind of voice for as long as I've known him.

We used to sing songs during commercials and try to harmonize but I was always the better singer which made Charlie jealous. Charlie always wanted to sing lead because he didn't know how to sing harmony. He said he didn't have the ear for harmony but I never believed him. He wanted to sing lead because it's the lead singer who gets all the glory. No one pays attention to the people singing harmony. In this way Charlie is like most people.

Anyone who isn't tone deaf can sing harmony.

The Charlie like most people isn't the same person as Charlie Robertson the hypothetical actor. How you can tell them apart is Charlie is real and the hypothetical actor isn't.

When we were kids I would call different kinds of people Charlie. Cops were Charlie Pork Chops or Charlie Nightsticks or Charlie Hambones. The ice cream man was Charlie Popsicle or Charlie Sundae and dogs were Charlie Canines or Charlie

Fleabags. I never had a Charlie name for MPs or security guards. I don't think I knew about MPs or security guards when I called everyone else Charlie.

Charlie didn't like it when I'd call these other people Charlie which is probably why I did it all the time.

Should the phone ring and it's Charlie I would know right off from the sound of his voice. Charlie is a baritone which proves my point. Baritones are never lead singers. Sure there are exceptions but not when it comes to Charlie and not when there's a tenor like me standing right beside him. This is how people tell us apart over the phone. There's no mistaking Charlie and me this way.

Should the phone ring it might be the smooth sounds of Charlie's silky tooth baritone.

That's how radio people would describe Charlie's voice.

When Mother called the house from work she knew right away which one of us had picked up by the sound of our voices. Whenever I picked up the phone she wouldn't say the hello how are you at all. She would say put Charlie on the phone like she had nothing to say to me herself. Once I asked Charlie why Mother wouldn't talk to me on the phone and he said what do you expect.

I don't know what Mother said to Charlie when he picked up the phone himself but I assume it was the hello how are you I'm fine I didn't sleep last night I have a headache.

Otherwise it was Mother saying to Charlie what do you want

for dinner tonight Charlie.

Charlie would say sandwiches and coleslaw would be fine.

Mother says you're not as dumb as you look Charlie.

Charlie doesn't say anything which is his way of saying thank you.

Mother says make sure your brother doesn't get hurt and die in the meantime.

Charlie says I am the responsible one Mother.

So people calling here expecting Charlie to answer should know it's not him as soon as I finish with the hello how are you. I know it wasn't Charlie who asked me for an allocution because Charlie was away at camp at the time and he wouldn't have known what a word like allocution meant anyway. Even with all the books he reads he wouldn't know a word like allocution.

Sometimes callers talk like I'm supposed to know what they are talking about. This is when I concentrate on the voice and leave the words alone. How the voice sounds is always more important than the words. Otherwise I tell them I have to go that I left something on the stove. Most callers don't know I don't have a stove here and can't leave anything on it.

Every morning during breakfast Mother would say she didn't sleep last night. She would come to the kitchen in her bathrobe and curlers and cook us breakfast. When she put the breakfast on the table is when she said she didn't sleep last night and she had a headache. She said but still I feed you rotten kids. We would both thank her by keeping our heads down and eating our breakfasts.

Breakfast was usually cereal and toast but sometimes it was eggs and other times pancakes. She would only cook eggs or pancakes if she wasn't running late which she almost always was.

I think this is when I started with the allergies.

Everything Mother cooked for us I was allergic to.

What happened was my stomach would be in agony and I'd have to go to the bathroom even more than usual.

Otherwise I would wheeze and it felt like I couldn't catch my breath. It was exactly like Charlie on one of our morning jogs only worse.

I would wheeze in my room and Mother would have to come in there to calm me down. She would give me a yellow pill and sing songs to me and before long I would stop wheezing and fall asleep.

This was Mother as an act of kindness.

Mother never noticed that for two whole summers Charlie didn't eat any of the breakfast she cooked for him. This was the time I made Charlie his drink of raw eggs and milk every morning when we got back from our jog. We had him on a special diet those two summers so he never ate Mother's breakfasts. What we'd do is when she turned her back we fed the breakfast to the dog.

Should the phone ring I will let the machine answer because I have arranged for the machine to answer after the eighth ring. I require patience from my callers from the people who dial those seven magic digits in the proper order or if it's from another area code then those ten magic digits in the proper order. It is rare for me to receive a call from outside this area code but it does happen sometimes. Usually it is a wrong number. I never hold it against the caller for dialing the wrong number and will usually say the hello how are you regardless. I don't know anyone from outside the area which is why it's always a wrong number from there. But always I let it ring eight rings so that the machine picks up.

Should the phone ring it might be time for my pills.

Sometimes they will call when it's time for my pills this way they won't interrupt when they come in here.

When they brought me my pills this morning I was in the middle of drawing a mother stick figure with her son stick figure in a doctor's office. The doctor was Indian and how I drew this is I had him wearing a headdress and smoking a peace pipe.

Upstairs was stick Charlie in stick intensive care. He was hooked up to all kinds of stick tubes and there was a stick hose in his mouth so he could breathe easy.

So the doctor gives me my pills like always and I ask him about my drawing. I ask him how do you like my drawing like that.

He said I was very talented so who could argue.

This is when I ask for more chalk. So far they've given me blue colored chalk and white colored chalk and I think it's

time for other colors.
I ask for an eraser too while I'm at it and he says I'll see what
I can do.

Mother saw what she could do when she did the Heimlich
maneuver on me. I was choking on a pink pill so I raised my
hand pointed to my throat and turned blue. She looked at
me and said let me see what I can do and did the maneuver.

The way they made these pink pills was so you'd choke on
them half the time.

What happened was after Mother maneuvered me I spit the
pill right out and we had to start all over again.

When all you have is a bed a table and some chairs you have
a lot of room to draw on. Without a television to watch
or radio to listen to there is nothing to distract you from
drawing either.

This is why I do most of the drawings naked.

Even if they've just brought me a fresh uniform I take it off
before I start drawing.

Only the first five or so stick figures were drawn with my
uniform on and I will probably erase those if they ever bring
me an eraser.

I don't think I can draw without being naked.

I don't know if other artists are the same way.

Yes my situation distracts me from drawing sometimes but I try not to let it bother me. If my situation needs attention I will give it the attention it needs and then go back to drawing. My situation only needs attention for a minute or two at a time so it's never a problem.

What bothers me is I've never thought to draw on floors or walls before.

Although Mother wouldn't have wanted me to draw stick figures in her house like that.

Mother would say what the fuck do you think you're doing. She'd say this is my house sonny boy not yours.
She'd say when you have your own house you can do as you please but until then I am the boss and you are subordinate to me in every way do you read me mister.

And if she caught me naked at the same time she'd say no one wants to see that either and of course she'd be right.

I have never had my own house unless you count here which I don't.

How you know this isn't my own house is there's no air conditioner or television.

I wouldn't have people watching me from the other side of the window though I would need someone to bring me my pills so I'm not sure how that would work.

If I had drawn in Mother's house I'm sure my drawings today

would be better that is if Mother didn't kill me for drawing in her house in the first place. This is something you get better at as you go like Charlie was with boxing. It took years for Charlie to become the boxer he eventually became and we were all so proud of him that day.

Sometimes my stick figures are crooked or cockeyed. Sometimes I have stick figures whose heads are too big for their bodies though you can't actually help that when you draw stick figures.

Sometimes I draw tic-tac-toe boards and I place Xs and Os in the squares like Charlie and I used to at the kitchen table. What I do is if Charlie is X in a certain game I will draw all those Xs left handed in honor of Charlie.

The left handed Xs are always crooked which is exactly how Charlie drew his own Xs.

Charlie had the worst penmanship in school and it's even worse now because he can't keep his hand from shaking.

Should the phone ring my heart might stop short and I might drop dead all over the floor here. That first ring always shocks me and my heart always stops short right after that first ring finishes ringing. I can never train myself to not be shocked by that first ring. I used to spend half my day expecting the phone to ring so I wouldn't be shocked by it. I stood next to the phone waiting for it to ring is how I tried to train myself.

This is why I think Mother was afraid I would get hurt and die. If the phone could do this to me imagine what Charlie could do inside a boxing ring.

I usually don't even hear the second and third rings because I am trying get my heartbeat back and catch my breath. The trouble is I hyperventilate when my heart stops short and when I hyperventilate I fall down. I'm not sure if this happens to other people but it has always happened to me this way. By the fifth ring I am back to normal unless the call comes in the middle of the night and then it takes until the seventh ring for normal to happen.

Otherwise it is after the fifth ring when I wonder who might be calling and why.

Sometimes it is a bullfight with myself whether to answer or not.

When that eighth ring finishes ringing and the machine picks up I walk around the room like I'm a matador and the phone is the dying bull. Another way to look at it is I am playing Charlie and the phone is me on the canvas. It is probably better to think of it this way because I raise my hands over my head and dance around the ring like Charlie used to do whenever he knocked me out. Charlie didn't win too many fights so whenever he did he made sure to enjoy it.

I've never seen an actual bullfight so I have no idea what the matador does after he stabs the bull to death. I don't think matadors dance around with their arms over their heads.

If you are not patient and cannot wait for the eight rings then please don't call me is what I'm saying.

Every time Charlie knocked me out I would make him beg

forgiveness. I would make him get on his hands and knees. I would say to him what the fuck did you knock me out like that for Charlie.

Should the phone ring I will not say the hello how are you but will instead say from what area are you calling me from. I've decided I will not accept calls from certain areas.

The machine itself was a gift from Mother. I can't remember if it was a birthday gift or a Christmas gift but right after she gave it to me she said we all have to make sacrifices.

We would hold hands and sacrifice ourselves every night before dinner.

This is something Charlie would have us do sometimes. Except with him we would hold hands around the dinner table while Charlie the fanatic prayed for everyone.

The trouble was Charlie didn't pray out loud so I never knew what he was praying for. I figured he was praying for our sandwiches and coleslaw and so that he might be a better boxer and Mother wouldn't get fired from her next job and finally that I wouldn't get hurt and die this way he wouldn't be responsible.

Mother and I would look at each other while Charlie prayed like this and it was like we were both saying to each other what the fuck is wrong with Charlie.

For two whole summers Charlie was a fanatic like this. He would stay in his room to read what he called the word of

God. We didn't watch television or box or do anything we normally did all the time. Charlie said we had to repent ourselves if we wanted salvation.

Charlie said he was born again and here was another two words I had trouble with.

This is when Mother sent Charlie away to camp for the first time.

Alabama Arizona Arkansas California Colorado Connecticut Delaware Florida Georgia Hawaii Idaho Illinois Indiana Iowa Kansas Kentucky Louisiana Maine Maryland Massachusetts Michigan Minnesota Mississippi Missouri Montana Nebraska Nevada New Hampshire New Jersey New Mexico New York North Carolina North Dakota Ohio Oklahoma Oregon Pennsylvania Rhode Island South Carolina South Dakota Tennessee Texas Utah Vermont Virginia Washington West Virginia Wisconsin Wyoming Asia Africa South America Antarctica Europe Australia are the areas I will not accept calls from.

Charlie and I would watch movies on bullfighters whenever there weren't any boxing movies. Usually there was a pretty girl the bullfighter was in love with. She was a peasant girl from a fishing village with fire red hair and flowing skirts and she would dance every night for the vatos at the cantina. The trouble was always the peasant girl's fisherman father. He never trusted the bullfighter and who could blame him. Charlie would have me do a bullfighter in love with a pretty peasant girl as one of my many performances.

I lahve you Maria Conchita Daniela Esposa. My blahd burns for you mi amore. I will kill this bull for you I will stab this bull many times so you will know how much I lahve you.

Charlie was on the floor whenever I did this for him.

I always used extra vibrato when I said I lahve you Maria Conchita Daniela Esposa like that.

I will only accept calls from Alaska from now on. This is because Alaska is where Charlie and I grew up and where Mother gave birth to us.

Should the phone ring I will keep tracing my hands on the walls instead of answering.

This morning I traced my left hand all over the wall opposite the table and chairs. I started tracing right after they brought me my pills.

The doctor said how are we this morning Johnny.
I said we're fine Johnny which means please stop talking.
Then the doctor said what are we going to do today Johnny.
I said we might trace our hands all over the walls in blue chalk Johnny.
The doctor said that sounds great Johnny we're doing fine here.

So now there are blue hands pointing up and down and in all directions in here. There are blue hands traced palm down and others traced palm up and I won't stop tracing blue hands until I fall over from glee.

I have hands with fingers spread out wide and hands with every combination of fingers spread out at different angles. Some of these hands look like the boy-scout salute and others like the A-OK signal.

Charlie was in the boy scouts for two whole summers until they kicked him out of it. What happened was he set some other boy scout's tent on fire when he was supposed to be pitching his own tent instead.

Mother gave Charlie hell for this and it was my job to make sure I didn't encourage him. She would say Charlie is punished until further notice and don't you encourage him like that.

I never encouraged Charlie to set anything on fire I don't think.

Even if Charlie was here right now I wouldn't encourage him to set here on fire.

I have two blue hands in here giving each other the finger. I put these hands in opposite corners so that they are facing each other. One of these has an extra long middle finger so if this was a contest you'd say he was the clear winner.

Why I did it this way is because Charlie's hands were always so much bigger than mine. We used to hold our hands up to each other and he'd laugh at me. Charlie said I had the hands of a little girl and this is when I'd give him the finger.

So there we were giving each other the finger in the living room and Mother would say what the fuck is wrong with you two. Sometimes I remember Mother with a drink of Scotch whisky in her hands and a cigarette burning between her lips.

I think Mother was a heavy smoker and drinker but not always. I think Charlie and I told her she couldn't smoke in the house anymore and what she said back was whose house do you think this is.

Even so I think Mother quit her smoking and drinking because I don't always remember her smoking and drinking all the time.

For instance whenever she came in to give me my pills at night she never smoked or drank.

She didn't smoke or drink when she was making us sandwiches and coleslaw either.

There are some hands traced in fists too though these don't look much like hands to me.

I wanted to draw two hands in a handshake but I don't know how to draw that so I tried to draw two hands locked in an arm wrestle like how Charlie and I used to arm wrestle each other at the kitchen table.

I always had the stronger arm and this like everything else made Charlie jealous.

Right next to that drawing I have a Mother stick figure smoking a stick cigarette and drinking a stick drink and in a drawing next to that one I have the same Mother stick figure quitting smoking and drinking for the last time.

How I have this stick figure quitting for the last time is her hands are on either side of her head like it's about to come off her shoulders.

Should the phone ring I won't stop the conversation with myself to answer. I think I have been in the middle of the conversation with myself for thirty-two years now. It is hard to mark the time when they won't let you have a clock for the wall or a television to watch.

The conversation with myself is never boring. When we were kids Mother said I was a lively conversationalist and I'm the same way with myself today.

Mother and I would discuss any number of things when I was a boy though most of them had to do with Charlie. What Charlie was doing and where Charlie was and why couldn't I be more like Charlie were some of her favorite topics.

When she said why I couldn't be more like Charlie she meant why did I have to be someone who would get hurt and die like that all the time.

When I am in the middle I never stop to answer the phone unless I think the caller might say something I haven't been saying to myself already. There is no way to know this beforehand which is why it is always a crapshoot to answer the phone when it rings.

The conversation with myself last night started with me saying a man died last night.

Then I asked how.
Then I said it doesn't matter because he is dead.
He is passed away.
Passed on.
Deceased.
Expired.
He is no longer with us.
He has bought the farm.
Checked out.
Cashed in.
He is deader than a doornail.
Headed for the happy hunting ground.
How.
He smoke'm peace pipe.
He is six feet under.
Down for the dirt nap.
Pushing up daisies.
Then I said how did he die.
I answered he did not feel well.
He was under the weather.
Not himself.
Not a happy camper.
Out of sorts.
Below par not up to snuff.
I asked myself what did he do.
I answered he sought medical attention.
He was better safe than sorry.
He was an ounce of prevention all over a pound of cure.
He checked himself in.
He had hesitated and lost.
Had one foot in the grave.
His days were numbered.

He was at death's door.
On thin ice.
He was treated aggressively.
Better late than never.
Locking the barn door.
So that's when he died I guessed.
No I said the treatments were successful.
It was a miracle.
He was a lucky man.
He was blessed.
He felt better.
He went home.
Counted his blessings.
Stopped and smelled the roses.
Took time for himself.
He went back to work.
Put his shoulder to the wheel so that his nose to the grindstone.
He went for a walk.
Went on vacation.
Saw the world.
Sowed oats.
Burned the candle at both ends.
Borrowed from Peter to pay Paul.
What happened next I said.
He went to the bathroom is what happened next.
He found blood I asked.
That's right I said.
I knew it I said back.
He cursed his maker
He went back to the doctor.
He had reaped what he sowed.

He was asking for it.
Tempted fate.
Pressed his luck.
What did they do I wondered.
I said he was treated aggressively but the treatments were unsuccessful this time.
He was past the point of rescue of no return.
And then.
He suffered.
I see.
He died.
So that's that I said.
I said no that's not that because before he died and before he got sick. Between the here and now and the happily ever after and the way back when. He was always more than one way to skin a cat. He was every dog having its day. He was quiet as a church mouse and all monkey see monkey do. Happy as a clam with a pig in shit and crazier than a fox in a henhouse. Ate like a horse and drank like a fish which was wise as an owl and stubborn as a mule. Ran around like a chicken without a head and naked as the day a jaybird was born. He was all or nothing. No in-between no happy medium. He was the polar opposite. He was the left hand not knowing the right. Cold as a witch's elbow and hot to trot at the same time. He was six on one hand half dozen on the other and finally in the end he was better the devil you know.
And now he is dead like a dead man.
At least he is not suffering I said.
He is at peace.
He is in a better place.
Watching over us.

I had this conversation with myself and the phone didn't ring once during it and even if it did.

How I knew a man died last night is I'm not as dumb as I look.

I tell this to the doctors when they come in to examine me. I say I'm not as dumb as I look like that. They almost never respond when I say this. Sometimes when one of them is examining me another one is in the corner reading the newspaper. He is sitting there with his legs crossed like he is on a park bench somewhere. I always tell this one to go fuck himself.

Should the phone ring I might let it keep ringing so that the machine answers because sometimes the machine will say you have reached me so please leave a name and number and a brief message. I never listen to the message whether it is brief or not. I figure there's nothing in the message that has anything to do with me so I don't listen to it.

My best hand is to the right of the window from where they watch me. What's different about this one is I didn't trace my left hand for this drawing. I wanted to see if I could draw a hand without tracing and it turns out I was right all along.

I concentrated on the chalk and the wall in front of me. I didn't think about my situation once while I was moving the chalk around and I didn't think about them watching me on the other side of the window either.

Sometimes I try to look through the window myself but it's

impossible. You have to be on the other side of this window to look through it although I have never been on the other side of the window myself. I might ask them when they bring me my pills later if I can see through the other side of the window but they would probably say no so why bother.

Up close I couldn't tell what I was drawing although I knew I wanted it to be a hand. The palm of this hand is thin and the fingers are long like Charlie's. I don't think I was trying to draw Charlie's hands on purpose but I'm not surprised it turned out that way.

I couldn't draw fingernails on any of the traced left hands but I came close with Charlie's hand. There are four imperfect ovals on four fingers and for Charlie that is good enough.

How you know they are Charlie's hands is because of the knuckles. Charlie had the ugliest knuckles you ever saw and the hands on the walls here are no different.

Charlie had to have broken each of his ten knuckles at least ten times during the course of his boxing career. We'd stuff padding inside his gloves but it never worked. We'd tape his hands up tight and that wouldn't work either.

This is why we had him drink raw eggs and milk all the time for the calcium. Charlie read that calcium was good for bones and we knew his bones needed all the help they could get.

Charlie was always breaking his bones so the raw eggs and milk didn't help at all.

Whenever I made him raw eggs and milk I'd tell him this is for your bones and he'd say but it tastes horrible and I'd say if you didn't have the bones of an old woman maybe things would be different.

Should the phone ring and it's Charlie I will say Charlie you have yourself a great hand on my wall.

Sometimes the doctors have me write poems to see how I'm doing. They tell me to express myself and I tell them it's hard to do when I chafe like this.

Sometimes the doctors want me in writing so I have no choice in the matter.

The poem I wrote last night was the best one yet.

The answering machine is like a sandwich.
My uniform is like coleslaw.
So what the fuck is wrong with the air conditioning.

The conversation with myself started when Charlie was away at camp. He was away two whole summers and it was me and Mother alone in the house without him. I remember being alone in the house with Mother and sweating and not having anyone to watch movies or boxing matches on Friday nights with. Mother said she couldn't afford air conditioning because her boss touched her inappropriately so she got herself fired instead. Mother said she didn't know what she was going to do with herself. I told her I was sweating and if I continued sweating I would dehydrate and die. I said

maybe she should think about that for a while.
This is when Mother gave me money for the ice cream truck.

The ice cream truck wasn't the same without Charlie behind
me running after it. I was always the faster runner even
though Charlie was older and responsible.

Whenever I would get to the ice cream truck without Charlie the
ice cream truck would say where is your brother Charlie today.
I would say it's just me today. I would say Charlie is at camp
getting better.
That must be nice for him truck said.
I said I wouldn't know and can I have a lousy Popsicle please.

I would explain to Mother why we needed air conditioning
every night during sandwiches and coleslaw. I would say
Injury Alaska is a desert in the summertime. I would say all of
downstate Alaska is a desert and people everywhere are dying
because of the lack of air conditioning. I would pull down my
pants to show her the chafed parts and say look at what you're
doing to me Mother. This is when Mother would say you hold
your situation young man and I will get you the powder.

Should the phone ring it might be Charlie from camp. Charlie
would call us from camp a couple of times each summer to
let us know how he was. He was always good or if he wasn't
good he was getting better.

He never said what he was getting better at so I assumed it
was either boxing or meditating.

I pictured camp near a lake surrounded by a thick forest.

There were huts and barracks where the campers lived and a mess hall where they ate their meals and watched television. All the huts and barracks had air conditioning as did the mess hall. Charlie had two friends he would meditate and spar with. One was especially good at meditating and the other at boxing so it was always good for Charlie to be away at camp like that. The camp counselors lived in a nearby hotel and were paddled in every morning on blue canoes from up the lake somewhere.

These counselors wore white coats and clipboards and had the best air conditioners in all of Alaska back at their hotel. All of the campers hated them for that Charlie especially.

Mother didn't let me go to the same camp as Charlie. She said she couldn't afford it but maybe next summer I could go. I asked her if we could visit Charlie at camp and she said they didn't allow visitors so the answer was no.

I never went to Charlie's camp or any other camp for that matter.

Should the phone ring and it's Charlie from camp I will say the hello how are you and hear what he has to say for himself. One summer Charlie said that camp was strange and that he might want to come home instead.

I said the hello how are you and waited for a response.
Charlie from camp said it's Charlie from camp calling.
I said Charlie how is camp.
Charlie said camp is strange and I might want to come home instead.

I said what is strange about it Charlie.

Charlie said every Monday night she juggles. Lemons oranges rolled up socks it doesn't matter what she juggles it. We'll put a kazoo in her mouth and have her blow tunes like *You Are My Sunshine* or *The Tennessee Waltz*. She loves it and I am afraid of her.

I said why are you afraid of her Charlie.

Charlie said Tuesdays it's the guitar. She's all right until she tries finger picking but she gets frustrated and starts slapping herself in the head. Beer calms her down most nights. Then she'll strum and strum until she breaks a string or we take the guitar away from her.

I said they let you have beer there Charlie.

Charlie said Wednesday night is cabaret night. She'll do a striptease down to a g-string and pasties. She gets this animal look in her eyes and gets us worked up so all anyone wants to do is go off into their rooms and do what feels good.

I said like what the dog used to do when he humped on us Charlie.

Charlie said exactly like that.

I said to Charlie who are you talking about Charlie.

Charlie said the best is Thursday when she does her ventriloquist act. She has a puppet named Ginger dressed up as a prostitute. She swings a fox stole around with one hand and holds her hip with the other. She has a great ear like yours. I bet Mother would say the same thing if she were here.

I said maybe she wouldn't because she's unemployed again.

Then I said can you tell which ear is the great one Charlie.

Charlie said Fridays most of us take or leave. She tries to impersonate famous movie stars singers politicians but it gets boring and we fall asleep.

I said I didn't sleep so well last night Charlie. I was sweating and Mother still won't let us have an air conditioner.

Charlie said that sounds like Mother to me.

Charlie said Saturdays are quiet. A lot of us don't even show up Saturdays. She'll either pantomime or dance ballet. She's graceful and it makes her happy so why bother.

I said it's good she's happy Charlie.

Charlie said we mud wrestle Sundays. We dress her up in a bikini and she takes us on one by one and it goes on for hours.

This is when I asked Charlie when he was coming home.

Charlie said I have to go now it's lights out time.

I said okay Charlie but how are you doing.

Charlie said I'm getting better I think.

I said that's good Charlie and hung up in his face.

Maybe it was more than two summers in a row he was gone for or maybe it was years he was gone and not summers. I think it may've been years because I can remember being alone with Mother in the house more than I can remember being with Charlie and Mother in the house all at the same time.

The summers Charlie was away at camp were glorious. I could walk around the house and not worry about meditating or boxing. I didn't have to wake up early and tiptoe out of the house so as not to wake up Mother. The one time we did wake up Mother she yelled out what the fuck is going on out there and Charlie and I had to run back to our rooms and pretend we were sleeping. With Charlie gone I slept late every day like a normal kid. I didn't have to go jogging with Charlie and I didn't have to hold up the laundry bag so he could pummel it to death. I didn't have to make Charlie his breakfast drink and I didn't have to play games with him which he would never let me win anyway.

What I'd do instead is watch television all day long and do what felt good.

Regardless of how long it'd been I always recognized Charlie the minute he'd walk through the door. I always knew Charlie by how tall he was and by the blonde hair on his head. He'd come through the door and say hello to me and Mother and then the three of us would sit on the sofa and eat dinner together and watch the television. Mother would say how much taller he'd grown over the summer and then Charlie and me would sing songs during the commercials.

Another thing is they won't give me a television to watch in here. When I ask them about it they tell me they are tired of making sacrifices.

If I had a television to watch I'm certain I would get better right away. I'm certain it's the lack of television is what's wrong with me here. If I had one I would watch boxing and baseball and movies like Charlie and I used to do by ourselves.

I am probably the best in all of downstate Alaska at watching television.

Charlie and I would have contests to see who was better. The rules were you had to watch the television without getting up from the couch. You couldn't go to the kitchen for sandwiches and coleslaw and you couldn't go to the bathroom either.

My record was over nine hours which Charlie could never come close to. Charlie would get impatient and leave himself open like always.

Yesterday I drew a tic-tac-toe board on the wall and
challenged the doctor to a game. I said whoever wins gets
his own air conditioner.

I said I will even let you be X okay.

Should the phone ring I will say the hello how are you
and listen to the words that come back if there are words
or I will listen to the nothing that comes back if there is
nothing but what I won't do is sound like an MP or security
guard anymore. I have had it with security guards and MPs.
They are never outside my door patrolling up and down for
intruders especially when you need them.

Sometimes I measure myself against a wall like Mother
did with Charlie and me when we were kids. Every year
Mother would have us stand with our backs to her closet
wall and she would mark in chalk how tall we were. She'd
mark Charlie in blue chalk and me in yellow and that's how
you could tell us apart.

Charlie was always taller because he was older and not sickly.

So here in this room I am not getting any taller which doesn't
surprise me.

I have always been too short for my own good.

It was always hard for me during our television watching
contests because I always had to go to the bathroom too
much. It's the same way here.

I can never spend the whole day drawing like I want to because I always have to interrupt myself to go to the bathroom. What happens is I knock twice on the window and this way they know to come in here and escort me to the bathroom.

They lead me down a dark corridor and into the bathroom and they wait outside the door for me just like Mother. Sometimes they even say are you okay in there and I tell them I'm busy I'll have to call them back.

They like it when I draw on the walls here. They like the hands especially and how I know this is they never come in here to stop me when I'm drawing.

The only time I tried meditating in here they came in to stop me which proves another point about these people.

What happened was after they brought me my morning pills I made my bed right after taking them. Usually I pick up a piece of chalk and start to draw after taking my pills so they must've known something was wrong.

My last drawing had a mother stick figure losing her job because her stick boss was cruel and unusual. How I drew this was I had the stick boss showing his stick situation to the mother stick figure and he says what do you think about this.

What I never do is make my bed in the morning because why bother and also I was never any good at making beds. Mother taught us how to make our own beds and this was probably the only thing Charlie was better at than me.

I had trouble lining up the sheets so that they weren't hanging over the sides and falling onto the floor. Charlie never had this problem himself but he had his own share of problems because after all this is Charlie we're talking about.

So I made my bed the best I could and yes the sheets were uneven but at least I tried. What I did next was sit on the bed like I used to on our living room sofa with Charlie whenever we meditated. I sat up straight exactly like Charlie taught me and closed my eyes and listened to the nothing.

I decided I was going to do this until I fell over from hunger or exhaustion or whatever it was that would make me fall over.

I had my eyes closed and listened to the nothing forever that morning and right in the middle of it is when they came in here and stopped me.

How they did this was four of them came in here and picked me up off the bed and sat me down in a chair. Then the doctor came in afterwards and asked me what I was doing and I said to him I was meditating so what's wrong with that.

He said we don't want you doing that here Johnny and he gave me another pill and the four who picked me up before picked me up again and put me back in bed and tucked me in goodnight.

Should the phone ring it might be camp on the other end. I will say hello camp how are you. Camp will ask to speak to Mother and I will ask to speak to Charlie. I will say what have you done with Charlie camp and why isn't he getting better. Camp will say put your Mother on the phone and I will tell camp to go fuck itself instead.

The bathroom here is nothing like the bathroom we had at home with Mother.

This bathroom has white tile and white walls and no shower inside it. There is a urinal and toilet and two sinks with hot and cold running water except it takes forever for the hot water to get hot.

We never had this problem at home and we had a shower and bathtub too.

How I take a shower here is they come in and give me a sponge bath instead. What happens is two of them hold me down and another one runs a sponge over my body. I tell them this is cruel and unusual which is probably why they seem to enjoy it.

They do this to me once a month.

I don't have a calendar or clock in here so I don't actually know how often they sponge me down.

They never do it how Mother used to when I was sick with fever. Whenever I was sick with fever Mother would sponge my head and chest to cool me off.

She never ran the sponge over my situation which is what they do here whenever they give me a sponge bath. I tell them have you no shame whenever they do this.

Whenever Charlie was away camp is where Mother said he was though I'm not sure it's true. I think Mother said Charlie was at camp to make me jealous. Otherwise she said it so I would behave more like Charlie myself. She used to say why can't you be more like your brother Charlie. I forget what I was doing when she would say this.

I was probably holding my situation to show her the chafed parts if I had to guess.

I think if I behaved more like Charlie then I too would be sent away to camp.

Meaning also that if I didn't chafe like Charlie and if camp was actually where Charlie was in the first place.

Also Mother didn't like it how allergic I was to the food she cooked for us. This is one of the reasons I was sickly growing up.

Charlie said he wore a special kind of cotton uniform at camp. He said they made everyone wear one whether they wanted to or not because they were all part of a team now. Charlie didn't like teams which is why he always meditated and boxed instead.

For instance Charlie only joined the baseball team that one summer. He said there wasn't enough violence in baseball and he didn't like having coaches and teammates.

Like me Charlie wasn't a good second basemen. Charlie

wasn't afraid of the ball killing him like I was but you wouldn't know that from the way he played. It was like he was trying to field a live grenade half the time.

The only time I wasn't embarrassed of Charlie as a second basemen was when he got beaned and charged the mound. First he threw the bat at the pitcher and then his helmet but both the bat and helmet missed because Charlie threw like a girl. This was another reason I was embarrassed to call him my brother.

So there's Charlie charging the mound and I'm yelling from the bleachers keep your goddamned left up this time Charlie.

That was the end of his baseball career and we both said good riddance to that on the way home.

But like me again Charlie looked especially handsome in his baseball uniform so we always had that to fall back on.

Charlie called his camp uniform a jumpsuit and he said it was the kind Chinese karate fighters would wear in the movies. I asked him once what color belt he was and he said they wouldn't let anyone wear belts so it didn't matter. I asked him how he kept his pants from falling down and he said that's why they make us wear jumpsuits instead.

Charlie didn't say if he sweated in that suit and I didn't ask because Charlie didn't like to talk about sweat. I asked him about sweat one time and he smacked me across the nose and said you shouldn't ask questions like that about people. So I don't know if he did sweat in that jumpsuit and if he did did he chafe too.

If he did chafe it was probably the counselors who brought him powder.

I can see Charlie holding his situation while some counselor in a white coat and clipboard applied the powder for him.

Charlie looking like he did on the canvas after a vicious knockout.

Charlie and I would watch karate movies whenever there weren't any boxing or bullfighting movies on for us. Charlie liked it how I could sound like one of those Chinese karate fighters because of my great ear. He was on the floor whenever I did a Chinese karate fighter for him. How I did this is I would bow to Charlie first and then rise up into a fancy karate move where I would kick with my right leg and land on my left all the while chopping the air with my bare hands. Then I would move my lips around fast and say something like asshole you have disgraced my sister's honor. The sister was always a peasant girl from a fishing village and the Chinese karate fighter was her older brother.

On the floor Charlie told me they didn't call each other asshole instead they said ah so you have disgraced my sister's honor.

He said he liked his jumpsuit because this way he didn't have to decide what to wear every day. He said it was comfortable and good for meditating in though he didn't meditate anymore. When I asked him why not he said it was none of my business.

Charlie would say it was none of my business right before going into his room to masturbate so I always knew what he meant by that.

This morning I drew a stick Charlie inside the ring with a stick Muhammed Ali. How you can tell it's Charlie is he is scared to death and how you can tell it's Muhammed Ali is he isn't.

I had Muhammed Ali dance rings around Charlie and then Charlie gets impatient like always and Ali knocks him out with a wicked combination. The next drawing has Charlie on the canvas and there's Ali dancing over him. He is taunting Charlie and who could blame him.

If you look off to the corner you can see stick me climbing through the ropes to wake Charlie up. I have a stick water bottle in my hand and I'm about to squirt Charlie and tell him he's lucky to be alive.

Saying I am in the middle of this conversation means the conversation will continue another thirty-two years or so I think.

I was never good at math and neither was Charlie so he couldn't help me with it. Mother made us do our homework together at the kitchen table every afternoon when we got home but she didn't like it when we asked for help. She said she already went to school and that part of her life was over. She said we had to figure it out on our own because that's how the world works. This is only when she was unemployed because when she wasn't she'd still be at work. Those days Charlie and I would watch the television together instead of doing homework like most normal kids our age. Then when Mother would come home with our sandwiches and coleslaw she'd ask did we do our homework and we always said yes we did.

I am probably two-thirds to three-quarters to almost done with the conversation with myself if you can believe that sort of thing without a calendar.

Should the phone ring I might let the machine answer because sometimes I arrange for the machine to say nothing when it answers. Sometimes I have the machine sound a long beep and then say nothing on the other side of the beep. Sometimes I want it that when people leave a message they might wonder if they've dialed the wrong number instead.

This nothing when the machine answers is similar to the nothing on the telephone and similar to dead air. This nothing goes on forever like before the earth without form and void.

I like to see how uncomfortable people are when they come across this nothing for the first time. It's like they don't know what to do with themselves. I sometimes listen to them leaving messages for me and I laugh until I hyperventilate and fall down. They don't know I am listening while they leave this message so it's even better. What they do is mumble the hello how are you and they sound like Mother gave them too many pills.

This morning when the phone rang was another story altogether.

I said the hello how are you and the doctor on the other end said this is another story altogether.

I said start from the beginning and don't leave anything out please.

The doctor said pay attention because I will not repeat myself.

I said make sure you speak slowly this way if I have to think about one word too long I won't miss too much.

The doctor said once there was a man who began every story with the phrase once there was a man.

I said to him how tedious.

The doctor said tedious indeed.

Then the doctor said this was a dull man witless and unoriginal. He was not a good friend to the few friends he had and his family had disowned him when he was quite young.

I said Mother tried to disown us herself but she lost the paperwork. I said this is why Mother was always getting fired all the time.

The doctor said listen to my story and hold thy tongue.

I said fine then where were we.

The doctor said this man was possessed of an undeniable charisma and his ability to weave a compelling narrative was unmatched. He could hold forth with kings and queens and as easily as anyone.

I said when I try to sound like anyone the caller hangs up on me.

The doctor said his audiences always knew what was coming with this plot turn or that one and they still could not tear themselves away.

I said my brother Charlie was a lot like this before the boxing.

Then the doctor said when he died no one mourned for him and no one attended what could only be described as a modest funeral. To this day his tombstone makes no mention of his incredible storytelling.

I said to the doctor why are you telling me this and the doctor said think about it and I will try you again tomorrow.

This is why should the phone ring tomorrow I will have another decision to make.

Unless I decide to stop forever with the words and concentrate on the voice.

The doctor has the kind of voice that makes you wish for too many pills.

Should the phone ring I will ignore it and continue the conversation with myself instead. Sometimes I will talk to Charlie in my head if I haven't spoken with him on the phone recently. The Charlie in my head is almost exactly like the Charlie on the phone. They are both of them tall and smart and more like Charlie used to be than he is now.

We might talk about how we used to watch television and sing songs together or how Mother would give us a dollar to chase after the ice cream truck at night and how we'd end up on the other side of the neighborhood for two lousy popsicles. Otherwise we talk about what I do here every day and how they took my clothes from me and won't give me a television to watch.

When I talk with him like this in my head I never stop so I can answer the phone. I almost never remember to check for messages either.

Sometimes if it is a wrong number I pretend I am the person

the caller intended to call. In other words I pretend to be an actor like the hypothetical Charlie Robertson playing summer stock in upstate Alaska somewhere.

After I answer they will say something like Hey Gracie it's Maggie calling and I'll say Hello Maggie how are you. Then I will ask about the kids and work because most people named Maggie have both kids and work. Sometimes they realize I'm not Gracie and when this happens I will ask if they are Gracie themselves. This is when I ask to speak to Gracie. I say Maggie put Gracie on the phone. I say what have you done to Gracie Maggie. This is when they usually hang up if I haven't done so first.

Should the phone ring I might answer it after the third ring. When I answer it after the first ring people wonder why I answered so quickly. They wonder if I was waiting for the phone to ring. They wonder if I was standing right next to the phone waiting for it to ring.

It is always a question of which ring to answer the phone after. Each ring means something different so you have to know beforehand who is calling.

If you pick up on the first ring it means you were standing right next to the phone hoping it would ring. You were saying please ring to the phone please ring right now please.

If you pick up on the second ring you probably don't want the caller to think this so you wait for the phone to ring a second time before answering. Waiting for the second ring almost never fools the caller because they know you were right there waiting for the phone to ring.

If you answer after the third ring this means you were somewhere else when the phone rang otherwise you were in the middle of a conversation with yourself and didn't want to interrupt by answering.

Four or five or six rings means it's a bullfight with yourself whether to answer and maybe you win this time and maybe you don't. Either way you dance around the room like the phone is Charlie on the canvas after you knocked him out with your own dangerous combination.

Otherwise they think maybe you don't want to talk that you didn't sleep last night and have a headache. There is nothing wrong with not wanting to talk or not sleeping last night or a headache.

Should the phone ring I will ask why it is I can't dial out anymore. Every time I pick up the phone to call someone now I never get to anymore. What happens is I pick up the phone and listen to the dial tone which is always there. Then I push the seven magic digits in the proper order and I wait to hear the ring on the other end which never happens anymore. The only thing I hear is the dial tone still. So should the phone ring this next time I will ask how come.

Should the phone ring I will answer it after the fifth ring and will say thank you for calling Charlie's take out service. I will ask the caller if they want a sandwich or coleslaw and then I will ask how they intend to pay for it.

Should the phone ring I will complain about the air

conditioning. I will say what is wrong with the air conditioning. I will tell the person on the other end that I am sweating and when I sweat I chafe and when I chafe the insides of my thighs are rubbed raw. I will say I cannot walk myself around anymore. I will say I cannot walk myself over to the phone anymore so there's no point in trying to call.

Should the phone ring I will answer it and ask to speak to Charlie. I haven't spoken to Charlie for so long now.

Should the phone ring I will continue doing what it is I'm doing. What I'm doing now is masturbating. I have been masturbating since early this morning. Sometimes I masturbate because there's nothing else to do here. If they gave me a television to watch I'd watch it and maybe then I could stop masturbating all the time. I think they want me to keep masturbating which is why they don't give me a television to watch. I think they watch me to see how many times I can masturbate. I think I am their television is another way of saying it.

There is probably a sofa on the other side of the window and they are watching me from this sofa and compiling data. I think I am part of a study about the relationship between masturbation and the lack of television. It may or may not have something to do with the phone always ringing too. Maybe they think the sound of the phone ringing makes me want to masturbate. I don't think this is true but maybe they think so anyway.

These doctors in their white coats and clipboards are not smart people. You can tell by how they mumble like Mother gave them too many pills. You can also tell how they're not good at helping people get better. Charlie's camp counselors were the same way and it was a tragedy what happened there.

Charlie was away at camp for two whole summers and always said he was getting better when we spoke on the phone but the truth was he never did.

I could tell the minute he walked through the door he wasn't any better.

Mother could tell too which is why she sat us down at the kitchen table that one time and asked what do we want to do with our lives. Charlie said it was either boxer or priest and I said as long as they have air conditioning I'll do anything.

Then we asked is that right Mother.
Mother said whatever you do don't become doctors in white coats and clipboards or camp counselors and everything will be fine.

Sometimes when I masturbate I do it because I am pretending to be Charlie at camp whenever he got worked up and would go off somewhere to do what felt good.

Last night when the phone rang it was words again. I said the hello how are you like I'm supposed to and all of a sudden they tell me this ugly story I never heard before.

This one wasn't a bullfight so I didn't dance around like Charlie before I answered. I say the hello how are you and right away comes the people on this train are an ugly story. I tell them I don't want to hear it this time Johnny.

They say it isn't up to you so shut the fuck up and listen.

I say fine then.

They say they all of them have ugly faces and hair and ugly shoes and feet and makeup and they read ugly books and they listen to ugly music on ugly headphones.

I say they probably come from ugly people who come from ugly people who came from an ugly place.

They say whether or not the people on this train are ugly of character is immaterial. What these people do to each other or to other people elsewhere doesn't concern us. Of the two physical ugliness is more objectionable but we do not say this out loud.

I say how could you Johnny.

They say when we look at each other we say with our eyes there is no faking this kind of ugly.

I say do you think Charlie is ugly.

They say I'm not talking about Charlie.

I say that's your problem right there.

They say we're not finished with the story Johnny.

They say what's worse or funny or some queer combination of the two is that when all the ugly people get off at this stop or that one even uglier people take their places. It seems like a mathematical or physiological impossibility.

I say both Charlie and I weren't good at math so we can't help you with that one.

They say we don't need help.

I say that's what you think Johnny.

They say it seems like something that happens to you when you're dead and you've done ugly things during an ugly life.

I say how could you again.

They say the people on this train are all manners of ugly.

I say how many of them exactly.

They say it would not serve to describe the ugliness in detail.
We know from ugly.
I say the doctors in their white coats and clipboards are
ugly too.
They say other than the pervasive ugliness there is nothing
noteworthy about this train ride. When our stop comes we
get off the ugly train to hurry homeward and we don't look
at the people who rush past to take our places.

This is when I said who is calling please and then I cursed
myself for saying it that way because who is calling please is
not what I want to do with myself on the phone.

So right after I said who is calling please I said shut the fuck
up Johnny like an MP or security guard would if they made
the mistake of saying who is calling please themselves.

The persons on the other end took a breath like Charlie had
jabbed them in the stomach and this is when I hung up in
their faces.

Right afterwards I masturbated myself to calm down. I always
masturbate to calm myself down and this was no exception.

Maybe I have been wired to want to masturbate whenever
the phone rings. When I frisk myself I don't find any wires
but maybe they put the wires on the inside. I frisk myself
to warm up before masturbating and have never found any
wires is how I know this.

Sometimes when I frisk myself I pretend I am a foreign
agent spying on Alaska and Charlie is the one who caught

me. So it's Charlie who frisks me when I pretend this and he arrests me and throws me in the cooler. This is when I bang on the door and say Charlie let me out I'll talk. I'll tell you whatever you want to know. Ordinarily it's only name rank and serial number but this time it'll be different. I tell Charlie through the door that I will tell them everything. Names dates bank account records the names of my superiors and a list of contacts inside Alaska.

Mother gave birth to Charlie and me in Injury Alaska.

Alaska the motherland Alaska the beautiful is what Charlie and I call it to this day.

The reason there might be wires inside me is I hear a high-pitched tone in my head and it never turns off. This tone sounds like the way old televisions used to squeak until you punched the top of them.

We had a television that would make this sound and Charlie and I would take turns punching the top of it. We would be on our sofa eating the dinner of sandwiches and coleslaw Mother brought home from the store and watching the television. We'd watch black and white movies or boxing matches on Friday nights. Otherwise Mother would pick out what we would watch because it was educational. She made us watch a bunch of movies about an African guinea man who got his foot chopped off next to a tree because it was educational. For two weeks I ran around the house saying kamby bolongo mean river until mother threatened me with the ladle.

We would sing songs for her during the commercials because

Mother liked it when we'd sing. Sometimes the songs were the actual commercial jingles and other times it was our own songs. Sometimes she would make us dance too because I was light on my feet. We'd both dance jigs while we made up our own songs to sing and almost always it was about the kamby bolongo and I was always the better singer which made Charlie jealous. He'd punch me in the stomach so I would stop singing and dancing better than him. This is when Charlie was more like Charlie used to be than he is now. Back when we were eating sandwiches and coleslaw and singing our songs while watching and punching the television and each other's stomachs to stop the noise.

I didn't used to hear this noise which is why I think it's possible there's wires in my head now. When I ask them about the wires they tell me to calm myself down.

In this case I don't think they mean I should masturbate but you can't always tell with them.

This noise in my head is like a horrible dial tone from a horrible phone that never shuts off. You can't dial out and there's no way to hook up an answering machine to it either.

I don't tell the doctors about the noise in my head because I think they're the ones responsible. I think if I told them about the noise they would say what noise we don't hear any noise.

The noise in my head is like the worst soprano singing the worst aria ever written. There is no vibrato and she can only sing that one high note and hold it until both of our heads come off our shoulders.

I can masturbate and masturbate and still this tone all the time.

Maybe they think the opposite that the sound of the phone ringing will make me stop masturbating. There is no telling what they want with me here. I will not stop masturbating to answer the phone. If they ask me this I will tell them otherwise they will have to learn it for themselves. Every time I stop masturbating to answer the phone I cannot concentrate on the words coming from the person on the other end and it is awkward. I don't like it when the hello how are you is awkward. This is most true if it is Mother on the other end.

Sometimes it was awkward when Mother applied the powder to the chafed parts. I would try to keep my situation out of the way but sometimes it didn't work.

Sometimes my situation would fall out in front of everyone.

Mother said what did we say about this young man.
I said I know Mother.
Mother said I think it's time you applied your own powder.
I said maybe it's time we got an air conditioner instead.

When I ask them why I can't dial out anymore they tell me to calm down or they tell me I'm doing fine. This is what they always tell me so I have to believe them.

Now that I think of it I think I was born with a headache. If I said otherwise I was mistaken and for that I'm sorry. I was probably given too many pills that day.

I think I remember now that I was born in the middle of a horrible fucking headache because of Mother.

Why I had this headache is I got stuck in Mother's tubes on the way out. This is why she always said what she said about giving birth to us.

Mother said the doctor had to go in with pliers to get me out. She said they had to clamp the pliers hard around my head and crushed my skull in the process.

She said she knew I was rotten from that very moment.
I said how was it my fault Mother.
She said it sure as hell wasn't mine.
I said how do you know.
She said the doctor said so.
I said since when do we believe what the doctors tell us.
She said the doctor said you had a bucket head and would never make yourself useful.
I said how could I do that Mother.

Then I said what about Charlie Mother how was he born.
She said at least Charlie had the sense not to have a bucket head and get stuck.
She said I should've had my tubes tied in the first place.

So it turns out I should've been more like Charlie even before I was born.

Or at least while I was getting myself born to the world through Mother's skinny tubes.

Why I have headaches all the time is the doctors crushed my skull the day I was born like the awful bastards they truly are.

I had to wear a special helmet whenever I left the house. I would be halfway out the door and Mother would scream from the kitchen to go get your fucking helmet.

Mother was afraid I'd hurt my head and die and who could blame her really.

For instance they made me wear a helmet when I played baseball that one year. Although I only got to play a few innings at second base and the rest of the time I was on the bench keeping score.

I was like an idiot out there at second base with a helmet on.

I also wore the helmet whenever Charlie and I went jogging with the dog. Here it was Charlie pulling us along and I was the idiot with the helmet on and that's how people could tell us apart.

Also Charlie was older and responsible and sometimes he had a crew-cut because he thought it made him look tough. Whenever he came home from camp he'd have a crew-cut and Mother would tell him he looked ridiculous like that.

Charlie looked ridiculous in his crew-cut and I was the idiot with the helmet.

This is why whenever we'd box Charlie would only pummel me in the stomach.

Everyone in Injury knew that my skull was crushed by the doctors and everyone felt sorry for me because of it. Every year they would have a radio-thon to raise money for my helmets and pills. Everyone knew that Mother was unemployed and couldn't afford my helmets and pills on her own.

One year they had me sing and do some of my many performances on the radio-thon. Mother and Charlie took me down to the studios of KINJ early in the morning so I could rehearse. Mother was especially excited and said this was my big break and I shouldn't blow it.

So what I did was the SS officer and the African guinea man and both the bullfighter in lahve with Maria Conchita Daniela Esposa and the Chinese Karate fighter saying asshole you have disgraced my sister's honor.

After that I sang a song about the kamby bolongo. Charlie and I had made up the song and the lyrics were the best we'd done.

Kamby Bolongo Mean River.
It don't mean liver.
Kamby Bolongo is my home.
It ain't never been Rome.
Don't be leavin' no plantation.
To hightail it back to your old guinea nation.
We'll tie you to a tree boy
Right over the root
Then tie up your ass and chop off your foot.

I sang it exactly like an African guinea man would and everyone said doesn't he have a great ear.

The radio DJ asked me questions like it was an interview right after the performance.

The DJ said that was lovely.
I said everyone knows that.
The DJ said we're here to raise money for you today.
I said I know that too.
He said last year we raised two thousand dollars and we're hoping for the same this year.
I said thank you because why bother anymore.
Then the DJ asked me how many helmets would I need this year.
I said it depends on how many times I lose one or Charlie steals one from me.
The DJ said Charlie is your brother is he not.
I said he is I think.
Then the DJ said is Charlie still boxing.
This is when I said nothing and instead let the dead air get all over everyone in the booth.

Everyone in Injury was on the floor after my performance and when they got up they all donated money so that I could have my helmets and pills like always.

This is how it is in Injury. I would walk down the streets and always there was someone coming up to me to make sure I was okay. Everyone in Injury thought I was going to get hurt and die right there on the sidewalk and no one wanted to see that happen.

These are the good people of Injury.

Mother is a lot like everyone else in Injury Alaska which is why she is probably still there.

Most everyone has two children and names one of them Charlie.

The people of Injury have their children sleep in opposite rooms and won't let them sit next to each other at the table. They make them play tic-tac-toe and they give them pills every night before they go to sleep.

They have them watch movies about the African guinea man because it's educational.

For two whole weeks everyone in Injury was either an African guinea man or overseer or slave catcher depending on if your name was Charlie or if your Mother was unemployed. So if you were a slave catcher and you saw an African guinea man running away you could tie him to a tree and chop his foot off for him.

The people of Injury would sing songs during the commercials and dance jigs all over the floor and would sometimes get themselves fired instead of working one job like normal people.

The people of Injury would gather at the kamby bolongo and sing and dance and chase after the ice cream truck on the other side of the river. At night almost everyone needs powder for the chafed parts.

If your skull was crushed by the doctors when you were getting yourself born the people of Injury are especially good to you.

Everyone listens to KINJ at night on their big fancy radios if they are Charlie and their small rotten transistors if they are me.

The people of Injury Alaska yearn for me.

Should the phone ring and it's Injury Alaska on the other end I will say the hello how are you and will tell the good people of Injury to hold on I'm coming.

Yesterday I drew a stick baby getting caught in his Mother's stick tubes. The Mother is on a table with her legs spread open and between them is a stick doctor with stick pliers about to crush the baby's head.

I never draw the good people of Injury Alaska. There is no way to capture them in stick figures and this is something we can all thank God for.

I might draw a stick figure masturbating in a room for a bunch of stick doctors on the other side of a window. I might have him picking up a bottle of baby oil in one drawing and then lying down on his bed passed out from exhaustion in the next.

Sometimes the wrong number is better than the right one. Sometimes it's not even a contest between right and wrong numbers. Sometimes it's like Charlie is the right number and I am the wrong one and Charlie has me up against the ropes and is pummeling me with body blows.

This is why God invented wrong numbers in the first place because he knew we couldn't ourselves.

Mother caught us one time in her room with me against the stole ropes and Charlie pummeling me into oblivion. She said what the fuck are you doing Charlie but Charlie was too busy pummeling me to hear so Mother climbed up into the ring and swatted him with her purse. This was Mother as the referee committing an act of kindness.

I think that was my birthday so right after Mother swatted Charlie we had a happy birthday cake in the kitchen together. Mother and Charlie sang the happy birthday song though I couldn't believe a word of it given what Mother said about how she gave birth to us.

The way they always sang the happy birthday song is Charlie would sing lead and Mother harmony which proves my point about Charlie again. When they were finished Charlie had to help me blow out the candles because I still had the wind knocked out of me from the pummeling.

The great thing about stick figures is you can make them do anything. I have an African guinea man stick figure running away from a plantation and into a thick stick forest. Behind him are two stick slave catchers on stick horses with stick bloodhounds running after him.

In the next drawing I have the stick slave catchers tying the stick guinea man to a tree and then I have them chopping his little stick foot off.

Should the phone ring I will ask for a clarification of the rules. I need to know what it is I can and cannot do again. Sometimes I think it's good they took my uniform from me because of the air conditioning and the sweat. But I think I might want some shorts to wear and I can't remember if shorts are allowed by the rules. The doctor who explained it to me mumbled like Mother gave him too many pills.

They didn't say why they took my uniform away from me when they took it away like that. I was in the middle of masturbating which made it awkward for some of them I think.

I remember the last time I got to wear my baseball uniform. It was the last day of the season and I was on the bench again because I might get hurt and die otherwise. They gave me a clipboard just like the doctors in white coats have and told me to keep score which I didn't know how to do. So what I did was play tic-tac-toe with myself instead. Mother and Charlie showed up and sat in the bleachers to watch me keep score like this for the last game. Mother was unemployed that day and Charlie was home from camp and both of them said look at the sacrifices we make for you.

I wore uniform number 31 that season because I was born on the 31st and the doctors needed 31 stitches for my skull after they crushed it. All the other players wore numbers 1-12 and I'd thought they wouldn't let me play because of my number. I thought maybe they didn't like it.

Then I remembered it was because I might get hurt and die if they let me play so it was good strategy on their part.

The truth was I wasn't a good second basemen regardless. I had trouble fielding grounders because I was afraid the ball would take a bad hop and kill me. I think all the talk about me getting hurt and dying turned me into a bad second basemen. I think I would've been a good one otherwise.

Charlie and I were the two worst second basemen to ever play second base.

The people of Injury Alaska gather every night at the kamby bolongo and await my return. They sing songs for me and bang on their drums a message for all to hear.

The message is return to the kamby bolongo o favorite son of Injury.

Should the phone ring it might be the caller who is trying to make me a millionaire. He doesn't say how he will make me a millionaire only that I should trust him and that if I sign up we can begin immediately. I tell him this sounds good to me so when can we start.

Should the phone ring it might be the caller who said I want to make love with a beautiful woman.
I said I think you have the wrong number myself.
Then the caller said not so much with her but to her at her in her general direction.
So I said in her vicinity.
The caller said that's a great idea and then hung up in my face.

Should this caller call back I will ask how it went and for every possible detail.

If the people of Injury knew I was here they would storm the gates and set me free. They would slay the MPs and security guards patrolling up and down for intruders and then they would murder the doctors in their white coats and clipboards.

Afterward they would carry me home on their shoulders and lay me down on the banks of the kamby bolongo. There I would bathe myself and enjoy a lavish homecoming with singing and dancing and sandwiches and coleslaw.

In the kamby bolongo I would soothe the chafed parts especially.

Mother taught us how to play tic-tac-toe at the kitchen table so we wouldn't bother her when she was eating. Mother liked it quiet when she was eating. She said she had a long day at work fending off her cruel and unusual boss who was a pervert. She said he showed her his situation right there in the middle of the office. She said he said what do you think about this and Mother said I think I'm fired again.

She said she couldn't stand the sight of his situation and this is why she wanted us quiet like that.

So what would happen at the table is Charlie and I would play tic-tac-toe without saying a word to each other about it. Since we weren't allowed to sit next to each other it wasn't easy to play but that didn't matter apparently. What we'd do is pass a notebook and pen back and forth the same as we would the sandwiches and coleslaw.

Mother would eat her sandwich and coleslaw and think about her day.

How we knew Mother was thinking about her day is I asked her once. I said what are you doing Mother and this is when she said I am thinking about my day. The way she said it was please stop talking and play your stupid fucking tic-tac-toe game.

Charlie and I never liked playing tic-tac-toe but we played anyway because why bother.

Should the phone ring I will rip the phone out of the wall this time. I will throw the phone on the floor and dance a jig all over it. I will dance and dance until one of them comes in here and makes me stop.

Sometimes when they don't like what I'm doing they come in here and make me stop. They never do this when I'm masturbating which is why I think they like it when I masturbate. Another reason I think they like it when I masturbate is they bring me baby oil to masturbate with. They do this so I won't chafe is what I think. I think if I were to chafe there it would undermine their experiments and then they won't get to come in here and make me stop whatever it is they don't want me to do.

How they make me stop is two of them will grab my arms and another two will grab my legs and the four of them will hold me aloft like I am on the rack. This is what it must feel like to be drawn and quartered is what I tell them but they always tell me to be quiet. Then I tell the two who grab my legs not to touch the part that's chafed. The insides of my thighs are rubbed raw because I sweat a lot and when I sweat too much I chafe. It is hard for me to walk myself around when this happens.

The reason I sweat too much is because of the air conditioning. I always tell the doctor who explains what I can and cannot do about the air conditioning but it never changes in here. The good thing is the men who hold my legs almost always remember not to touch the chafed parts. They might have to touch them in the initial struggle but they will not maintain a grip there. They will hold me like this until I calm down. I usually get upset for a while when they hold me like this. They tell me not to struggle but I forget sometimes and struggle anyway.

I also get upset with the phone sometimes. Always with the ringing and the dial tone but not being able to dial out and the words and the hello how are you and I'm fine I have a headache today I'm busy I have to go now I have something on the stove can I call you back I will leave you a message.

I love air conditioning the same way I love answering machines and uniforms. As long as we have these three things in the world everything is fine.

God was a genius the day he invented air conditioning.

It was very hot that day and God was sweating. Why it was hot is because a fire kindled in his anger and it would burn unto the lowest hell and shall consume the earth with her increase and set on fire the foundations of the mountains.

I don't know why God was angry that day but it could've been because of Charlie. Charlie always made Mother angry so why would God be any different. Mother would catch Charlie doing something she didn't like like pummeling me against her stole ropes or punching me in the stomach because I was always the better singer and she would say to Charlie goddamned you Charlie and maybe God himself heard that and did what Mother said.

So when God said he would heap mischiefs upon them and spend his arrows upon them he probably meant Charlie more than anyone else. So when he said they shall be burnt with hunger and devoured with burning heat and bitter destruction what he meant was Charlie shall be burnt with hunger and devoured with burning heat and bitter destruction.

I saw this after I'd give Charlie his breakfast drink of raw eggs and milk. He would come out of the bathroom after throwing up and say to me I'm starving hungry and need sandwiches and coleslaw and this is when I'd tell him that he was in training. He would say but I'm sick and I would press my hand to his forehead and sure enough he was burning with fever.

So when God got angry at Charlie and the fire kindled in his anger he did what he did with the burning heat and destruction and then said to Charlie look at what you made me do Charlie.

Charlie probably had that stupid look on his face like after I'd knock him out with a dangerous combination.

This is why God had to invent air conditioning it was because of Charlie.

Charlie the brilliant bastard responsible like always.
Sometimes Charlie and I would sit in the living room and sweat instead of meditating. This is because it was too hot to do anything else and still Mother wouldn't get us an air conditioner.

When she came home that day we spoke to her about the air conditioning. We said Mother we need an air conditioner in here and if we don't get one soon we don't know what. Then I told her I was sweating and when I sweat too much I chafe and when I chafe the insides of my thighs are rubbed raw. Charlie said he's right as a way of agreeing with me but before she could answer I kept on saying if I keep sweating like this I will dehydrate and die and is that what you want Mother.

I don't remember what Mother said to this but it wouldn't surprise me if she said we all have to make sacrifices so the answer is no. She probably said millions of people don't have air conditioning and for millions of years people didn't have air conditioning so why don't you make yourself useful and shut the fuck up.

This is another reason we can all thank God that we weren't one of the poor bastards who lived in a world without air conditioning before air conditioning. You wonder how people survived without air conditioning before air conditioning. You wonder if people had to drink extra water so they wouldn't dehydrate and die from all the sweating.

You wonder how much powder people needed back then.

Charlie and I would have to sit naked in our living room because it was too hot otherwise. We promised not to look at each other's situations though sometimes we couldn't help it. Charlie's situation was like the rest of him meaning you looked at it and said whatever.

It was so hot sometimes Charlie called it an inferno which it certainly was. He said it's like purgatory and Hades in here combined. He said we should all get used to it because the judgment was coming and this was like a preview of the everlasting hereafter.

Charlie Charlie Charlie is what I'd say whenever he'd say things like that.

There is almost no way to draw a stick air conditioner. I have tried many times and it never comes out right.

I want to draw the perfect stick air conditioner this way when the doctor comes in here next I can point to it and say what does that remind you of.

Charlie and I also watched submarine movies because sometimes you can't find boxing or Chinese karate movies on and you have to do something.

We'd pretend we were submariners ourselves and we'd say things like reverse the starboard engines and man overboard port side.

Charlie said he might want to join the navy and I told him he had no chance. Charlie couldn't swim and you can't have someone like that in the navy.

We were so crazy for submarine movies that I would tell Charlie to keep his port up instead of saying keep your left up. I would scream from the corner watch out for an overhand starboard but even then Charlie would get himself knocked out instead of doing what I said.

The doctor who comes in here has a white coat and clipboard and I can never understand what he says to me half the time. Sometimes it's because of the words and the rest of the time it's his voice. His voice is like a horrible air conditioner that makes more noise than it blows out cold air. It's the kind of air conditioner that sounds like torture it sounds like a bird flew into the back of the air conditioner and is being ripped apart in there. Whenever this happens the air conditioner doesn't work the way it should which is my point exactly.

This is how the doctor's voice sounds to me half the time.

Should the phone ring I hope it's Charlie. I have spoken the hello how are you with too many callers since the last time I spoke with him. I am ready now to do it with Charlie.

When they let me leave here I want to return to my native home of Injury Alaska alongside the banks of the kamby bolongo.

Back to my people waiting for me.

Charlie and I would sometimes go down to the kamby bolongo to fish and swim instead of training or meditating. What we'd do is wake up while it was still dark out and tiptoe out of the house even though Mother wasn't home most of the time anyway. For two whole summers Mother wasn't home at all. What happened was one day Charlie and I were on the living room couch watching the movie about the African guinea man and waiting for Mother to come home and bring us our sandwiches and coleslaw and what happened was she never did.

Charlie and I watched the whole movie because Mother liked to come home and test us to see if we were paying attention. She would say I want you two to pay attention to the movie instead of fooling around. According to Mother boxing and meditating was fooling around so why bother. She would ask us who the African guinea man was and we'd tell her his African guinea name and then his real one. Then she'd ask us what would happen to the slaves when they ran away and we'd tell her they'd get their feet chopped off or they would get tied to the whipping post and whipped. She also wanted to know why it was important we watch this so we'd tell her why and she would say that's wrong don't you two know anything and we would say we're sorry Mother but we don't.

Those two summers Mother wasn't home were glorious. Charlie and I could wake up whenever we wanted which usually meant after noon because we were always up late watching movies. Then for breakfast we'd make sandwiches and coleslaw instead of raw eggs and milk because by this time Charlie's boxing career was finished. Charlie was washed up as a boxer because he couldn't keep his head and hands from shaking all the time.

So what we'd do is I made the sandwiches and Charlie made the coleslaw. Mother had taught us how to do this once in case something happened to her. She sat us down at the kitchen table after dinner one time and told us we had to learn how to survive on our own if something happened to her. We said what was going to happen to you Mother and she said she didn't know but it was possible. She said the world was cruel and unusual so we'd have to carry on without her.

After our breakfast of sandwiches and coleslaw we'd sit on the couch and watch television until it was time to go to bed again.

We never went to school because Charlie and I didn't like school and school didn't like us in return. Our teachers would punish us with their sticks and send us home. This is why Mother made us watch the movie about the African guinea man in the first place because it was educational. She said do I have to educate you too on top of being the Mother all the time. She would go to school to yell at the teachers for sending us home. She would say I am the Mother not the school. I gave birth to these two and you are supposed to teach them how to be cruel and unusual.

Mother said to us I don't think I am being unreasonable am I.

Charlie and I knew she didn't expect us to answer so we kept our heads down and let her finish. Sometimes it seemed like Mother was asking us questions but she really wasn't. It was hard to know the difference which is why it was always better to keep your head down. This is when she cursed the school itself and said everything in the world is cruel and unusual and we'll probably all end up on the street someday.

I wanted to ask Mother what street we would end up on but then I realized who I was talking to.

There are holes in the ceiling of this room which remind me of the holes in the ceiling of my bedroom growing up. Sometimes I would count the holes in every tile instead of trying to fall asleep. Sometimes I wouldn't let myself fall asleep until I counted the holes in every tile.

I do the same thing here because I'm not getting any better.

Even when they tell me I'm doing fine and it's nice I'm not sure it is.

This is when I think I might be the African guinea man myself.

The men who hold me aloft are the overseers and the MPs and security guards are the slave catchers who tied me to a tree and chopped off my foot.

Before that happened I was snatched from the trees and sold into slavery and these doctors are the ones who bought me at auction. I was on the platform and the doctors inspected me by combing through my curly hair and checking my gums. I don't know how much they paid for me but I knew right then I had to start making myself useful.

Instead of sleeping in a barn and chopping cotton all day I sleep in here and masturbate.

What happened was one night after I finished masturbating the doctor came in to give me my pills like always but instead of making the pill circle or square disappear I tricked him instead. How I did this was I hid the pills under my tongue instead of swallowing them. I had done this with Mother once or twice so I knew what I was doing. It always worked because I'd swallow the water and said ah right afterwards like always.

Then I pretended to fall asleep and waited for the doctor to get up and leave. Sometimes the doctor waits for me to fall asleep but not the same as Mother did. For instance I don't have to lay still and twitch myself to get him to leave like I had to with Mother.

How he waits for me to fall asleep is he sits himself in the corner and reads the newspaper while I am pretending to fall asleep.

So after all this happened and he finally left I escaped through the tunnel under my bed.

I'd been digging this tunnel from the first night they put me in here. What I'd do is whenever I knew they weren't watching me masturbate I would secretly dig the tunnel.

The trick was hiding all the dirt from the tunnel but I knew how to do this because Charlie and I would watch prison movies whenever there wasn't anything else on. Our favorite was one where a bunch of prisoners dug three tunnels and escaped right in front of all the SS officers. These SS officers were like most MPs or security guards patrolling up and down except in this case they patrolled for prisoners escaping rather than intruders as no one would intrude on a prison camp I don't think.

So like those prisoners I hid the dirt on the floor and would mix it in with the dirt already there. The floors here are especially dirty so these idiot doctors never seemed to notice. I don't think the African guinea man on television had to dig a tunnel to escape. That is how you can tell us apart. I think he found a rock so he could saw off the shackles they put on him and had to drag around all the time. I think he sawed and sawed for two years before he could do this and it was the same way with me and the tunnel. It took me years to dig the tunnel but what else was there to do other than dig and masturbate all the time.

Although neither of us had a calendar so you don't know for sure.

They based the television guinea man on me and everyone knows it.

All they did was change a few details because that's what you have to do to make it educational.

The trouble was I didn't get too far once I got out of the tunnel. I was trying to find my way back to the kamby bolongo but I got lost instead. I didn't know which direction to run in and I didn't have Charlie to run along with me so after a while I got tired and why bother.

This is when the slave catchers caught me and tied me to the tree. They said we have vays of making you talk and I told them everything they wanted to know which didn't seem to make a difference.

I didn't like it when they chopped my foot off for me but we all have to make sacrifices.

Should the phone ring I will let it ring and ring and ring. I will disconnect the machine from the phone so that it won't answer. There won't be any voice that says to leave a name and number and a brief message and there won't be a long beep with nothing on the other side of it. Whoever it is that calls will wonder why the machine doesn't pick up. They might wonder if there's something wrong with me if I've done something to myself.

The last time I did something to myself the phone rang and rang and I think it may've been Charlie who was probably worried about me doing something to myself which is probably why he called in the first place.

Charlie and I would swim up and down the kamby bolongo instead of going to school. I was always the better swimmer which made Charlie jealous. It was hard for Charlie to swim because of how his head and hands shook so I'd have to save him from drowning all the time. I'd be doing laps up and down the kamby bolongo and would look behind me to find Charlie and he'd be gone. This is when I'd have to dive under to find him at the bottom and pull him up. I'd drag him to the shore and pound on his chest so that he'd cough up all the water he swallowed. It was a lot like how I'd go into the ring after some boxer knocked him out because he forgot to keep his portside up.

Should the phone ring I will answer it and start singing songs into the receiver and I won't stop singing until I fall over from glee.

We would always bring the dog to the kamby bolongo because if we left him in the house he'd probably die from the no air conditioning. I would hold the dog's leash while Charlie jogged and pulled the two of us along. Charlie was still a good jogger despite all the horrible shit that happened to him. When we'd get to the bolongo I'd play with the dog for a while though sometimes the dog was afraid of the water like Charlie was. I would throw a stick into the water and the dog would look at me instead of fetching it himself. The way he looked at me was why did you throw that stick into the bolongo if you wanted me to bring it right back to you.

This is how I am with the doctor in his white coat and clipboard. I play his games and they tell me I am doing fine and I ask about the air conditioning or a clarification of the rules and he looks at me like Charlie just drowned in the kamby bolongo and it was my fault.

Sometimes I call the doctor massa because what's the difference.

Every time Charlie drowned in the kamby bolongo I'd drag him to shore and punch his lights out so he'd cough up all the river water he swallowed. Afterwards he'd thank me and we'd go for ice cream so it was never something to worry about.

The ice cream truck was on the other side of the kamby bolongo so we'd have to cross it every time. Charlie would be scared like when he had to fight an especially tough boxer and I'd call him a chickenshit palooka. This is when Charlie would get angry with me and start pummeling me in the stomach so I'd know he was ready to go out and fight only in this case it was cross the bolongo and not drown.

What happened was I found a shallow place to cross the bolongo so Charlie wouldn't drown and everything was fine.

We ate ice cream every night for dinner instead of sandwiches and coleslaw when Mother was gone. I remember us talking about Mother and where she might be.

I said to Charlie where do you think Mother is Charlie.
Charlie said I don't know.
Do you think she is coming back I said to Charlie.
Charlie said I don't know.
I said to Charlie do you think she wants to come back at least.
Again Charlie said I don't know.

Finally I said do you think maybe we should go look for her and you know what Charlie said to that so why bother. This is when I said to Charlie don't you know anything Charlie. Then I said what the fuck is wrong with you Charlie.

Then I would tell Charlie to make himself useful and get us more ice cream.

There are two ways to do something to yourself if you want to. The first takes about a week to do properly but it's the least bother by far.

The first thing you have to do is not take the pills when the doctor gives them to you. What happens is the doctor makes a pill circle or square on his hand. This is what he always does and you can't blame doctors for being doctors anymore than you can blame dogs for being dogs because they can't help it either. If Mother taught me anything this is what she taught me.

So you take each pill off his hand one at a time and place it under your tongue. The trick is instead of swallowing the pill you swallow only the water leaving the pill under your tongue. It helps if you say ah like you always do this way the doctor won't get suspicious. After you do this with every pill in the circle or square you wait for the doctor to leave. Maybe you have to twitch yourself once or twice or maybe you don't it doesn't matter. Once he's gone you take the pills from under your tongue and hide them under your pillow.

It's even better if your pillows and sheets are the same color as your pills because this way it's like camouflage.

You do this every day for a week and then when no one's trying to watch you masturbate you swallow every pill under your pillow at the same time.

This is the best way to do something to yourself if you want to.

So far two things happen when I do this to myself and neither of them is good unfortunately.

The first is I fall asleep and then I wake up because my stomach feels like Charlie has been pummeling it into oblivion. I am sweating even more than usual and then I have to throw up like Charlie used to when I gave him the raw eggs and milk. I throw up for a long time and then I feel better but I am even more dehydrated than usual and they have to give me fluids.

Then the doctors come in here and take my uniform from me and they take my pillow from me too because they know that's where I hid all the pills.

Whenever they do this I tell them they're not as dumb as they look.

The second way to do something to yourself is to take off your helmet and ram your head into the wall over and over.

This way doesn't work as well for two reasons.

The first is it gives you a horrible fucking headache every time. It doesn't matter what part of your head you ram into the wall either.

The second reason is even if you know they're not trying to watch you masturbate they can hear you ramming your head into the wall so they rush right in and make you stop. Most times you can only get three or four rams in before this happens.

Then four of them come in and hold you aloft with each one holding a separate limb. You say this is what it feels like to be drawn and quartered and they say why do you make us do this to you.

This time they fasten your helmet onto your head so you can't take it off and they tie your body to the bed so you can't get up. They tie down your arms and legs so you can't do anything with yourself.

You can't even masturbate which serves them right.

Should the phone ring I will say the hello how are you and not give the person on the other end a chance to answer. I will follow up the hello how are you with I'm not feeling well today the insides of my thighs are rubbed raw and I can't walk myself around anymore and this morning I finally thought to rub the baby oil on the chafed parts and that brought some relief but it doesn't change that my brother Charlie is who knows where and my hand hurts from all the masturbating and I don't know if the ice cream truck will come around again.

Then if the person on the other end is still there I will ask if they are the ice cream truck and why won't they come around.

This is another thing my hand hurts now. I don't think they care about my hand hurting is what I think. This is why I think these doctors are cruel and unusual because I know they want me to masturbate in the first place. They are the ones who don't give me a television to watch and they are the ones who give me baby oil so I won't chafe. Maybe I could live with my hand like this if I had a television to watch or if the phone could dial out but certainly not otherwise.

I tell this to the doctor with the white coat and clipboard so that maybe he might give me something for my hand but all he does is write it down on his clipboard and say I am getting better.

I don't know if he means I am getting better at masturbating or what. I know they watch me masturbate and compile the data but I don't know if I am getting better at it. To me I've always been a good masturbator.

I tell them I can't draw with my hand like this.

This is why I don't think this doctor is a real doctor. I think he might be the original Charlie Robertson playing the part of the doctor. I think this might be summer stock is another way of saying what I'm saying.

Last week I finally had a conversation with this hypothetical doctor and it proves my point.

The hypothetical doctor said how are we doing today Johnny. I said I'm doing fine Massa how are you.

This is the calling each other Johnny game we sometimes have to play except now I call him Massa instead.

The hypothetical doctor said my doctor wants me to walk and my wife wants me to walk so I go for walks now. I walk along the sound's shoreline which curves and bends its way into a row of houses on either side of the walkway. A retaining wall keeps the water from the road and from the houses on the other side of the road. It's hard to imagine waves tall enough to reach one or the other.

I said to him this is what happens when you don't get killed off in your prime Massa.

I said the doctors and wives conspire against you and make you do these things.

Then the hypothetical doctor said sometimes my legs burn when I exert myself so sometimes the walk takes longer than it should. When this happens I'll find a bench and look out across the sound and wait until the burning stops. The burning starts when I feel my calves tighten and then it's like I've got scotch whiskey instead of blood flowing from my knees down into my ankles.

I said this is exactly how my hand feels when I masturbate.

The hypothetical doctor said I didn't mention my legs burning to the doctor. I'm not someone who likes to tell people what's wrong with me. I told my wife over dinner and now my wife thinks I'm dying.

She sounds a lot like my brother Charlie I said to him next.

The hypothetical doctor said my wife says I'm going to die from cancer. I don't have cancer but my wife thinks I'll die from it anyway. She says it'll be my prostate or liver or colon. She doesn't say how she knows this but she says it'll be horrible. She says she doesn't want to spoon-feed me soup and sponge my body down and change my soiled underclothes to watch me die like that.

I'm not sure that's what happens to you when you get cancer but I pretend otherwise for the sake of conversation.

So I said is that so Massa.

The hypothetical doctor said when she says this to me I sing back to her *I don't have a husband he don't play the trombone.* She laughs when I do this.

That sounds like what me and Charlie would do for Mother during the commercials except most of our songs were about the kamby bolongo until Mother would threaten us with a ladle is what I said back to him.

Then I said how is your vibrato holding up.

The hypothetical doctor said what I mean to say is I'm not sure walking will keep any of that god awful business from happening or if the burning in my legs means the cancer has already started. My wife is a good woman and I don't want her to have to go through that business to watch me die like that. I don't care what happens to the doctor or what he has to go through.

I said I know what you mean by that.

The hypothetical doctor said then we look at each other like we've been married for twenty-five years with no end in sight. It's a nice moment between us. This is when she tells me to go for a walk after our dinner of broiled chicken and mashed potatoes and that I should eat more vegetables. Then we talk about the retaining wall and the road and the houses along the shore and I pick up where I left off after *he don't play the trombone.* We both start laughing this time and we don't stop until after the food gets cold.

I said it sounds exactly like me and Charlie except what we had for dinner was sandwiches and coleslaw and ice cream but only when Mother was away those two summers.

I told him I would draw a special picture for him. I said the next time you come in here remind me and I'll show it to you.

My idea for his special picture is to draw a stick doctor walking along the sound's shoreline and then dying of cancer right on the spot.

Now I can't wait to draw it and I can't wait to show it to the awful bastard.

This is when I know this doctor isn't a real one because why would he need another doctor himself. This is probably why he doesn't help me with my hand. He doesn't know how to help me because he's not real.

Every so often he comes in here and gives me my pills anyway. They don't say what the pills are for but they say I need them. I ask them where do you get these pills but they never answer me. I know the pills aren't for my hand because my hand never gets any better.

If I didn't take these pills I think I might get hurt and die. Or I think that's what I'm supposed to think and who can argue.

The one who gives me my pills now doesn't make a pill circle or square like Mother used to and I wouldn't make it disappear if he tried.

When I take the pills I ask does he know how to do the Heimlich maneuver just in case.

Should the phone ring I might answer it and say go fuck yourself. If it's Mother on the other end I will be sorry but if it isn't then whoever it is can go fuck themselves including Charlie.

Should the phone ring it might be Mother's lawyer from when she was on trial for her life.

Why Mother was on trial is she stole money from her boss although they didn't call it stealing they called it embezzling. This was another instance where I had trouble with the words.

Mother would have her lawyer over for dinner to discuss her legal strategy. The way they did this was Charlie and I would have our sandwiches and coleslaw first so that we'd be finished by the time the lawyer came over. This is when Mother gave us money for the ice cream truck except it was the lawyer himself who gave us the money because Mother was broke again.

Mother's legal strategy was a lot like Charlie's boxing. She was supposed to be patient and keep her left up but what happened was she was too aggressive and got herself knocked out with a dangerous combination.

What the fuck kind of word is embezzling is what I asked Mother one time and she said tell me about it.

Should the phone ring I might cry out for Charlie and I will keep talking to Charlie whether it's Charlie on the other end or not. I will ask Charlie questions and will tell him about the doctor who comes by and tells me what I can and cannot do. I will tell him about the phone and the machine and the songs I sing sometimes and how that I'm getting better. My range is improving so that I can hit the high A now which is respectable for someone who never made it in show business.

Mother was disappointed that I didn't make it in show business. I told her it wasn't my fault and she said well whose fault was it and of course she was right.

Should the phone ring I will let the machine pick up because I have arranged for the machine to tell everyone but Mother to go fuck themselves.

I haven't spoken to anyone on the phone or in person for weeks now. I think it's weeks but it could just as well be months or years. There's no telling time in here so you can never tell.

The doctor who explains what I can and cannot do hasn't been by to do that nor have the four men who hold me aloft been by to do what it is they do for a long time now. Maybe they have forgotten about me or maybe they have found someone else to do these things to.

The doctor who explains what I can and cannot do has arranged it so that the phone can only receive calls and not place any. I cannot call anyone from this phone is what I'm probably saying here.

I cannot tell anyone what the five men have been doing to me and I can't tell anyone that it seems they've stopped doing it to me anymore. I have picked up the phone maybe two thousand times and punched in every combination of numbers I can figure. There are no magic digits to dial so I can make a call myself is another way of saying it.

Should the phone ring I will ask Mother to call Charlie herself. I don't see why I have to be the conduit between them anymore. I will explain to her about the air conditioning and the chafing and the ice cream truck and then I will tell her I have something on the stove.

The trouble is I can't help it what they say to each other particularly when I'm not there.

Should the phone ring I might say why hast thou forsaken me O Charlie. Then I might say you was my brother Charlie you should've looked after me a little. Then he might say that I saw some action and then I'll say something about the short end dives and taking Wilson apart. That we could've taken Wilson apart that night in the Garden and finally when it's over I'll say it is accomplished Charlie.

Should the phone ring I will stop masturbating and answer it. I hope it's a woman that calls so she can talk to me while I finish masturbating. It is always better to talk to a woman while masturbating. I hope she has a nice voice and knows all the right words to say. It's not the same if I have to tell her what to say all the time and both of us know this.

This is only true if the woman is not Mother. There is no way to talk to Mother and masturbate at the same time.

Sometimes women call here and trick me into masturbating. This was back when the phone used to ring every so often and I was trying not to masturbate all the time.

I made a resolution with myself to only masturbate twice a day. What I'd do is I'd masturbate in the morning after my pills and then I would think about something else all day until I could masturbate again at night after the nighttime pills.

So all day long I would think about the kamby bolongo and the good people of Injury Alaska who can all go fuck themselves if they're not coming here to set me free.

Why I wanted to only masturbate twice a day is because my hand was killing me during this time. I couldn't masturbate more than twice a day if I tried which I certainly did.

My fingers were stiff and I couldn't move them anymore and my wrist felt like it was broken again.

I broke my wrist the first time on Charlie's jaw when he had me pinned against the stole ropes in Mother's room. He was pummeling me pretty good so I threw an uppercut and broke my wrist on his glass jaw.

Charlie fell to the canvas and I had to squirt water on him to wake him up. I told him next time keep your fucking left up and this won't happen.

Then Mother came home and I had to tell her I broke my wrist breaking Charlie's jaw with an uppercut. She said why can't that kid ever keep his fucking left up.

So the phone would ring and I would tell myself you are not going to masturbate no matter what happens next. Then after the hello how are you comes a woman's voice asking me if I want a subscription to the daily newspaper and I'd have no choice.

What I think was the doctors saw me only masturbating twice a day and this was undermining their experiments. They had this woman call me because they know I am not getting any better.

Should the phone ring I will tell Mother once and for all to stop calling me all the goddamned time. I will say the doctor comes by once a month to tell me what I can and cannot do and I have the phone and the machine and the long beep but no television to watch like the time you made me and Charlie watch that show about the African guinea man who ran away and got his foot chopped off next to a tree and then I would sing songs about the African guinea man until you made me stop with your ladle and I'll finish by saying if Charlie does call I'll tell him you said the hello how are you and that he should call more often. Past that I still masturbate all the time because what else do they expect me to do.

Should the phone ring I will answer it at once and I will say the hello how are you and listen to the words that come back. If the words that come back come from a woman's voice I will keep listening but I will not masturbate and if the words come from a man's voice I will probably hang up instead.

Sometimes I think there is nothing here that is worth the getting out of bed for and it's a real bullfight on those days.

Should the phone ring I will ask Charlie why he and Mother put me here. I will ask him if it has anything to do with the African guinea man who got his foot chopped off. I remember when I made up a song about the African guinea man and his foot Charlie and Mother yelled at me with a ladle and told me to stop. I will ask Charlie if he still sings songs during the commercials anymore. I will ask why have they conspired against me and for how long will this continue. I will ask what it is I have done. Is it because Charlie is jealous of me is that it Charlie.

Should the phone ring I will say kamby bolongo mean river right into it. Then we'll see what the person on the other end has to say about that.

Sometimes I think about the nothing all day but I never meditate anymore. It is too quiet in here to meditate without a television to watch or the phone ringing all the time.

Sometimes I pretend I'm Charlie in here and I talk out loud about the nothing and how this is what we are trying to get back to. This was God's plan all along is how I put it.

I move my eyebrows up and down like Charlie and say for ages there was only the nothing and nothing else. In the beginning there was nothing and it was good. It was good like this a long time until the nothing was interrupted by the advent of animals and people.

They never come in here when I do this because why bother.

Should the phone ring my heart will stop short because it hasn't rung in weeks or months now. I will probably fall down and hyperventilate if the phone should ring so it's probably good that it doesn't anymore.

Should the phone ring I will pick it up and say say something and I'll draw it. I will say keep in mind I only have blue and white chalk and can only draw stick figures.

Yesterday I drew a stick massa combing through the hair of a stick guinea man.

Should the phone ring I think I will drop dead all over the floor because it hasn't rung since I don't know when anymore. I think the last time I said the hello how are you was three or four years ago now. They never tell me what time it is in here. When I ask them what time it is they say I shouldn't worry about things like that. When I ask them to bring me a television to watch or a clock for the wall they say why bother. This is when I feel like I will never masturbate for their benefit again.

Should the phone ring I will keep talking with myself instead because the phone never rings anymore anyway.

Should the phone ring I will answer it and explain why I think I masturbate as much as I do now. I think it's because they took my uniform from me and that I'm naked all the time. There's nothing impeding myself from myself here. There's nothing to distract me from myself either. If I had a television to watch then maybe yes or if I had my uniform pants to wear then maybe yes again but there is no television and I have no pants.

It's always right there in front of me is another way of saying what I'm saying.

I don't know why they took my uniform from me that first day. One of them said it was so I wouldn't do something to myself but I didn't believe him.

I have never done something to myself with my uniform and I wouldn't know how to either.

The doctor who tells me what I can and cannot do wasn't the one who took my uniform. The four that hold me aloft like I am on the rack is who took my uniform from me. The doctor was somewhere else when they did this to me but I'm sure he was the one who told them to take my uniform in the first place.

The doctor probably dialed Mother and Charlie on the phone right after and told them I'm getting better.

I don't know what Mother and Charlie said back to him but it probably had something to do with sacrifices and then they probably told the doctor to give me their regards.

Mother and Charlie have always been this way so you can't blame them for it.

Should the phone ring I will say I am in here with no uniform and no television to watch.

I will say my wrist is broken and my fingers stiff and the baby oil isn't working.

I will say I will continue to masturbate until they tell me otherwise.

I will say there are two ways to do something to yourself if you want to.

I will say the words are important less than half the time and it's better to listen to what's between the words and behind them.

I will say for ages there was nothing and it was good.

I will say this is what we are trying to return to and that it was God's plan all along.

I will say there is a difference between meditating and masturbating but not by much.

I will say Charlie Robertson is upstate playing summer stock as a vicious military policeman patrolling for intruders.

I will say there is no end to what stick figures can do on a wall.

I will say Indians can't help being Indians any more than doctors or dogs.

I will say that kamby bolongo mean river and the kamby bolongo flows through the big broken heart of Injury Alaska.

I will say do not get caught up in your Mother's tubes or you will have a headache for life.

I will say I will return to the good people of Injury as they are waiting for me.

I will say keep your left up lest you be felled by a dangerous combination.

I will sing hosanna to answering machines and uniforms and air conditioners even though I don't have one in here and probably never will.

I will say I am sweating now and when I sweat too much I chafe and when I chafe the insides of my thighs are rubbed raw.

I will say thank God for inventing powder and that he was a genius the day he did that.

I will say whatever comes to mind about Charlie and Mother and everything that has happened since we were children watching television and singing songs and chasing after the ice cream truck.

I will say please keep Charlie and Mother in your prayers tonight and give them my regards when you see them.

I will say you are who you are and where you are and I am who I am and where I am so let's stop now with the hello how are you I have a headache and don't feel like talking so please leave a message because I am fine.

That's what I'll say should the phone ever ring again this next time.

I will say I am fine which means please stop talking.

The author gratefully acknowledges Sam Ligon, Amy Albracht, Toni Lopez, Dan Wickett, Steven Gillis and Steven Seighman.